The Sweet Void of Space

Alderbrian Press

Other books by Philip Raymond Sadler:

Asblin's Magic Cave

Azophi's Wand

The War of the Thirteen Enchantments

The Yarrow Enigma

Wild Wilkenson and The Man in the Moon Prophecy

Suggestions of Stained Glass
Flower Window Art
A coloring book.

Suggestions of Stained Glass
Abstract Art
A coloring book.

Books by Philip Raymond Sadler and T. D. Sadler:

Never Trust a Cricket

Wizards War

Published by Alderbrian Press.

Books by T. D. Sadler:

The House of Other Worlds

The Reluctant Hero

Wherever the Road Leads

Published by Famulus Press.

Alderbrian Press

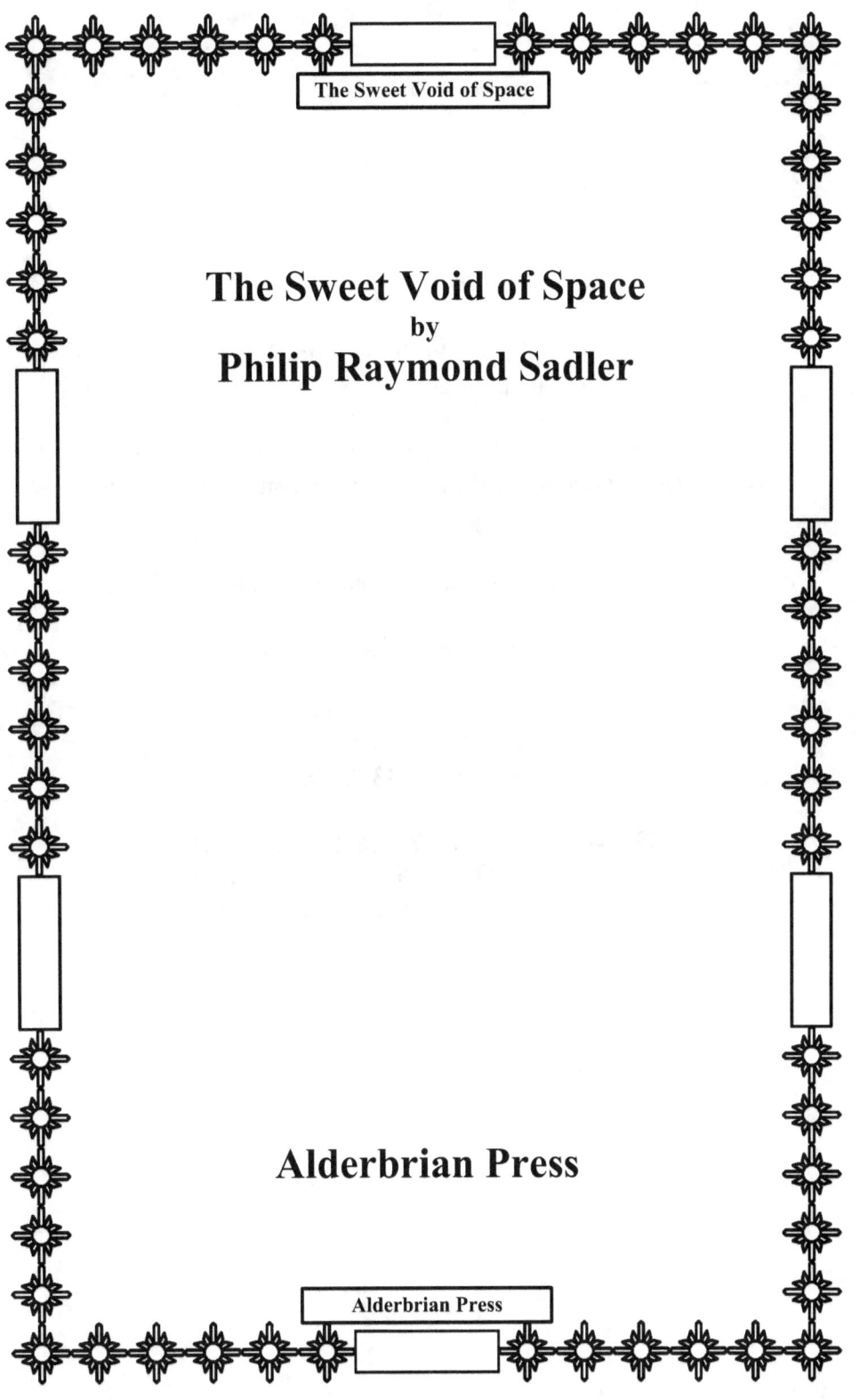

The Sweet Void of Space

The Sweet Void of Space
by
Philip Raymond Sadler

Alderbrian Press

Alderbrian Press

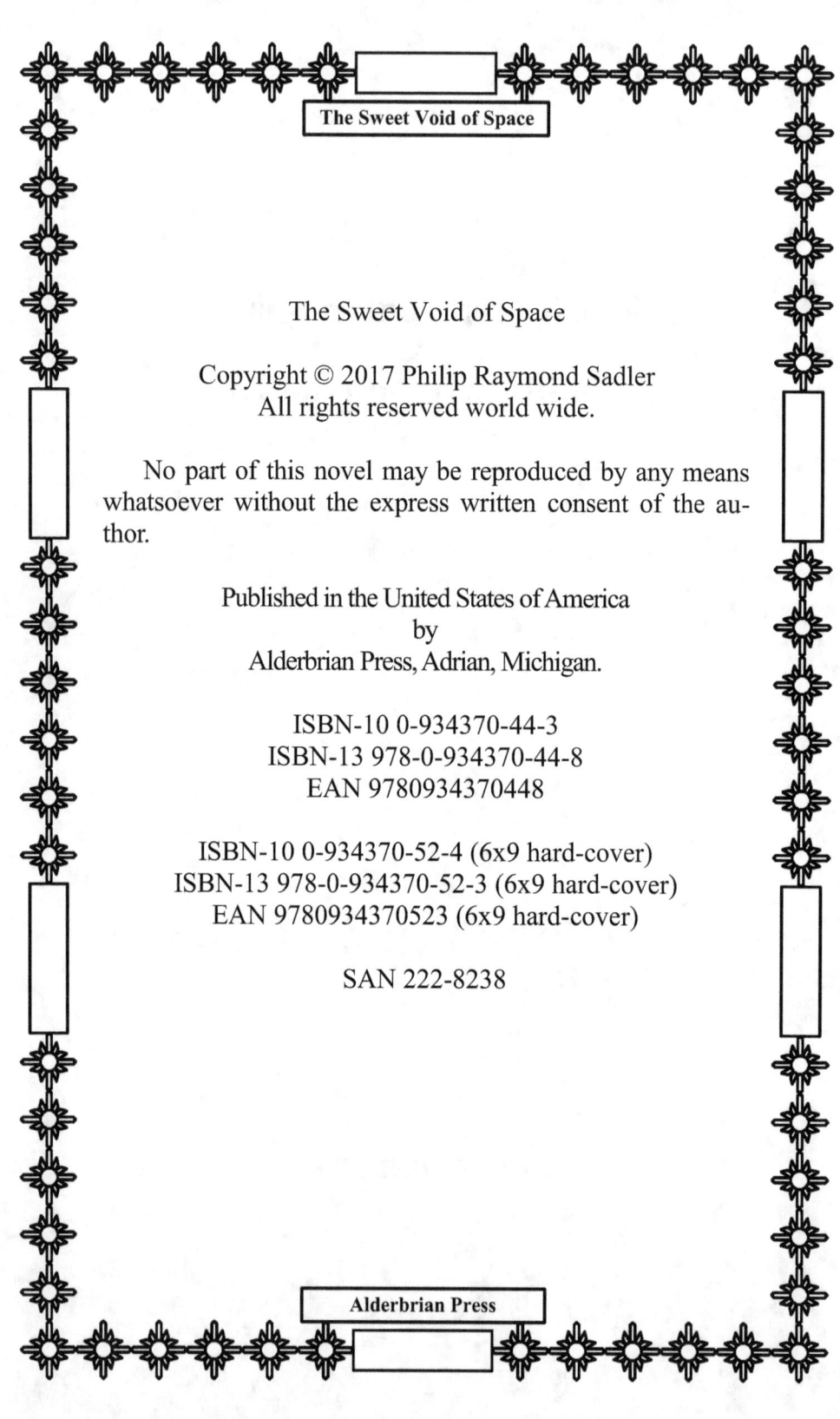

The Sweet Void of Space

Published in the United States of America
by
Alderbrian Press, Adrian, Michigan.

ISBN-10 0-934370-44-3
ISBN-13 978-0-934370-44-8
EAN 9780934370448

ISBN-10 0-934370-52-4 (6x9 hard-cover)
ISBN-13 978-0-934370-52-3 (6x9 hard-cover)
EAN 9780934370523 (6x9 hard-cover)

SAN 222-8238

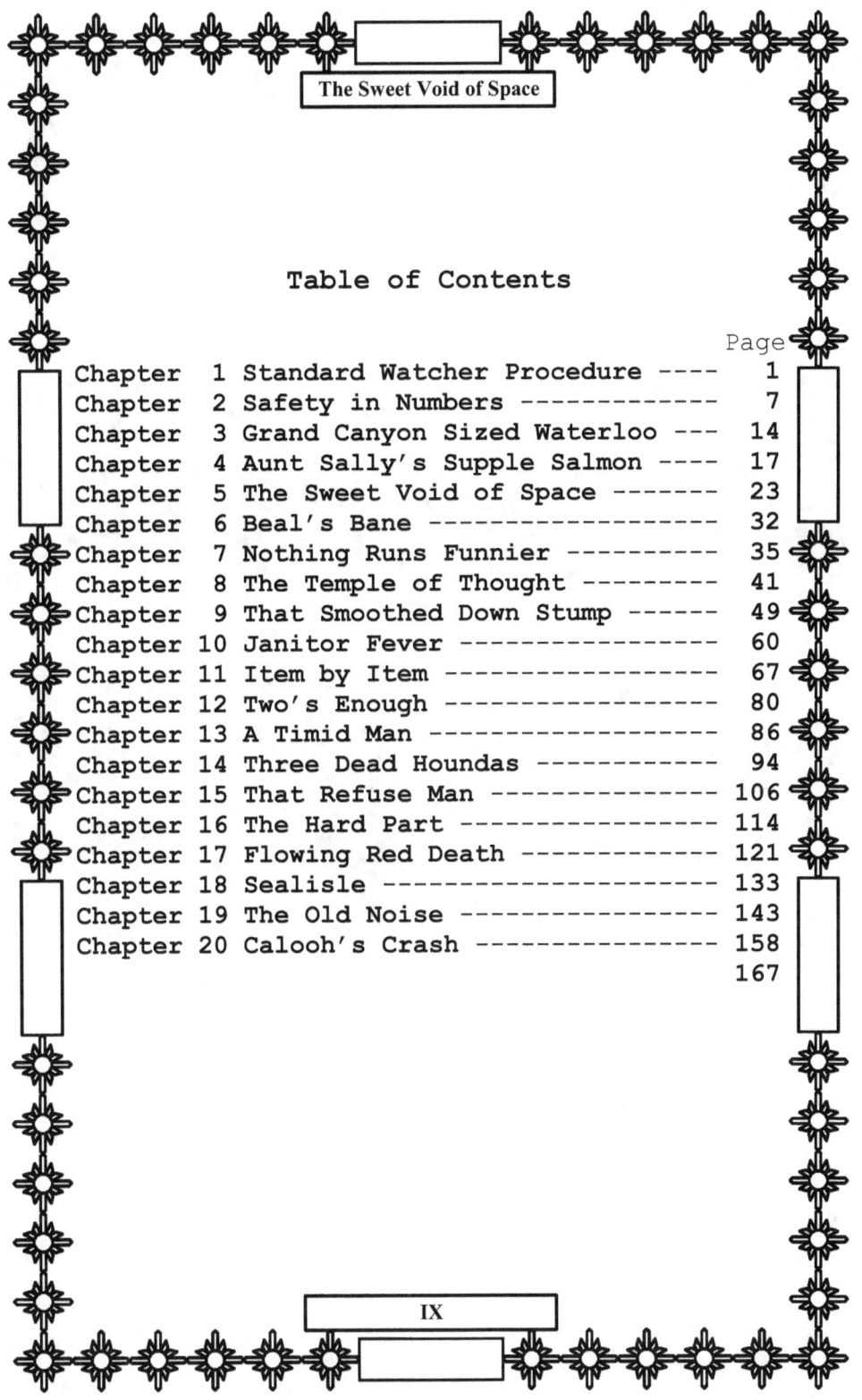

Table of Contents

Chapter 1

Standard Watcher Procedure

The closet of the weathered, but well maintained, log cabin was vibrating and humming. These phenomena ceased. The door unlocked itself with a loud click and slowly swung open.

The bright white light filling the teleportation chamber was provided by ceiling panels surrounding a round, flat, clear Transmission Crystal.

A great white bird stood in the center of the chamber. It had a Human-sized head, two large brown eyes, an orange beak and owl type ears. Its long, thick neck led to a swan-like body, big wings, slender orange legs and wide webbed feet, with short, black claws. Its weight was about thirty-six pounds. If it had carried more bulk, it would have been unable to fly, even with its huge wing span.

A man stepped into the strange fowl's line of sight and aimed a double barreled shotgun at his visitor's chest.

The ivory bird riveted its eyes to the weapon. "You *are* Timmorey?" it quavered.

"Yes."

"I *am* Assistant Administrator Calooh."

"Yes."

"Is that armament *necessary*?" Calooh said.

"Standard Procedure," Timmorey said. "You should *know* that." He took a step forward.

Calooh backed up, with the forefinger of his small, but strong, white, human-like wing-hand poised over the Recycle Button on the panel beside him. "The origin of Aloevongi Trees is interesting," he said, with hesitation.

"Things from the myths of the natives of planets other than our own are always more fascinating than our legends," Timmorey said evenly.

"All right," Calooh said, a bit less tense, "we've played the game, and both passed."

"If you're satisfied, come in," Timmorey said. He lowered the shotgun and settled into a hickory chair.

Calooh stalked from the chamber and perched on a three legged stool, facing Timmorey. The haughty bird was obviously alien. And Timmorey? Well, Timmorey was different also.

Calooh distastefully surveyed the cabin. The Teleportation Chamber stood to his right, in the corner, behind him. Opposite it, was what appeared to be a bathroom, with its door ajar. Behind Timmorey, there was a box of kindling and a fireplace of sooty, red bricks. A wooden rack, for the weapon the man held, hung above the marble mantle piece.

Opposite the hearth, was the cabin door. A metal bracket jutted out of the log walls on either side, about man-waist high. A wooden beam leaned beside the left bracket.

There were two windows in that wall, covered by thick, green, cloth curtains. Under the window to the right of the door, was a small writing desk, with a chair. A bookcase, filled with ledgers, stood to the right of this, and against the wall.

The room also contained a cot, a chest of drawers, a bottle-gas grill, four more chairs like that in which the man sat, but around a tiny dining table, a large built-in sink, which was probably used for cleaning eating utensils, and an animal skin rug. A bear, Earthlings called it.

Calooh turned his attention to Timmorey. He was perhaps, twenty-five or thirty. Rather young, for a Junior Grade Watcher. But Calooh always experienced difficulty judging the ages of aliens.

Timmorey's hair was dark brown, short and neatly preened—combed. His face was weather tanned. His green eyes showed—Pride—Intelligence—Authority? Something, undefinable, but important. A well-trimmed beard covered his chin and ran up into his sideburns. A mustache adorned his upper lip, coming down to meet the beard. He was of average Human stature and his movements said he had a well developed and toned body. He was wearing a checked, flannel shirt, blue jeans and tan boots.

Timmorey saw Calooh had finished his sizing up. So had Timmorey. He spoke first: "Why have you come? I told Operations, the Item I have, is a minor one, and of no real importance to them. They—or shall I say—you, possess a sufficient number of Items to contain the Gellnian problem until it can be corrected. I will not surrender this one to you."

The bird flapped off the stool. He became physically ugly as he spoke: "Operations did not inform me of this!" He trotted back and forth. "*I must have that Item*! I—They *said* you had been *ordered* to cede it to me!"

"Yes, and I have replied that I will not. Although you are second in command at Operations, Calooh, you are neither, worthy, nor loyal."

Calooh sucked air between small, even teeth set in pink gums. "You would *defy* your *superiors*?"

Timmorey made no reply.

Calooh flicked his tongue. "You shall regret life if you fail to perform as instructed!"

Timmorey stood. His expression showed he would allow no threats.

Calooh flinched.

"You may as well return to Operations," Timmorey said. "I shall see to it, the Items you have stolen, at such a grave time, shall be freed to their *true* purpose."

Calooh bobbed and snaked his head. "*You* shall see? A Watcher on Probation! And an *Earthling*, at that!"

Timmorey smiled humorlessly.

A lengthy hostile moment passed.

Calooh cleared his long throat. "*I* shall see that *you* are *penalized* for this *insolence*," he said. "As *painful* a *punishment* as *possible!*"

"I've no doubt you'll *try*," Timmorey said.

Calooh stalked into the lighted chamber.

Timmorey noted the bird had a mind-linked, miniature levitation device strapped to his back. It was the same color as his feathers and nearly hidden by his folded wings. Most Pharsey's used such devices. The birds were not known for self-control when it came to food, and were too overweight to fly without the assistance of the Levitron Belts. Calooh was not obese, so Timmorey assumed the bird used the Levitron Belt when he needed to carry heavy loads during flight.

Calooh glared at Timmorey. "I'll be back! And I'll bring something which will help me bend you to my every wish!"

"Don't bother," Timmorey said. "You wouldn't want to provide the stuffing for a pillow, *would* you?"

Calooh hissed with rage. He stabbed the forefinger of his left wing hand against the Recycle Button on the chamber panel. The Transmission Crystal was energized. It brightened the illumination in the cabinet, and he vanished.

Timmorey chuckled and watched the porter door close and lock itself with a loud click. He sat in the chair at the desk, pulled a ledger from the bookcase, took a ballpoint pen from the right hand drawer, and began recording the incident in absolute detail and honesty, as prescribed by Standard Watcher Procedure.

***

Timmorey returned the ledger to the book case. It was dark out now, the birds were twittering themselves to sleep, and it was high time for dinner.

Although the door was locked, he shoved the hickory beam into its brackets for added security.

He tossed some wood into the fireplace, added some rags he had used to clean his shotgun, fished matches from his pocket, and lit the fuel.

He stepped away from the cheerful fire and flipped the head of the grizzly bear rug back on the tail.

This revealed the three foot square trap door of a storage basement of plain earth. It contained some gardening tools, hidden controls and maintenance gear for the teleporter, a month's supply of canned goods, and at least one precious secret.

He opened the door, rubbed his hands together, with relish, and went down to select his meal.

Chapter 2
Safety in Numbers

Operations Central was a huge complex of filing cabinets, computer terminals, wastepaper baskets, dispensers of cheap food, and bubbly water coolers.

The employees of Operations liked to eat. When none of the big bosses were in evidence, they liked to sleep.

Bill Wayden had his feet propped on his desk. He was snoring and dreaming of girls.

The Director of Operations Central exploded through one of the five sets of double doors arranged oddly around Headquarters Section. He never waited until the autos kicked in.

Bill's feet hit the pig-colored tile floor, jolting him to groggy wakefulness.

Director Beal pointed at one of the thousands of filing cabinets. "So called Secretary, find me the folio on *Timmorey*! And *hop to it*!" he ordered, and blustered into his seldom used office.

Bill started fumbling in the file cabinet drawer marked: TIM. "Somebody must'uv stolen his pink undershorts to get him so ghouled up," he muttered. "Blubb in here and destroy a man's *leisure* fun *just* because he's the Big Word in the Shack!"

He stumbled across the correct folder, opened it and twisted up his face. The so called file consisted of a fourth of a sheet of paper darkened by two meager paragraphs of very simple words.

If he knew Beal, and he did, Beal would blame the strange paucity of information on little old Bill and break him to Janitor, again.

Not that a Janitor's life wasn't interesting. And, while one was a cleaner, one did enjoy free hospitalization and funeral costs in the event of a mishap to oneself. But he still did not look forward to another near stint at the—job.

Bill knocked on the Director's portal. Praying mentally, he entered, holding the paper at arm's length.

When Beal caught sight of the memo, he looked like a lean animal about to spring for the easiest kill in history.

Bill assumed as deep an expression of puzzlement and abject sorrow as he could, outdoing his old record.

Beal drew a long breath, not fooled by Bill's facial gymnastics. He snatched the scrap, ran his beady eyes over it twice, and looked up. "Have you ever been a *Janitor*?" he said.

Bill choked, crossed the fingers of both hands behind his back and began sweating. He thought about the legion of Janitors who reportedly never returned from the Refuse Room. He started trembling.

Beal handed him the slip. "Read this and tell *me* you can't dredge up anything else on the man!" he said.

Bill took longer than necessary.

TIMMOREY, ----------, born on Earth, educated at Earth University of Michigan, contacted by Watcher Harric Winters of Pepple and established as Watcher of Earth.

His Watch is reported uneventful and, as yet, unimportant to any part of Operations Central or Galaxy Control.

Bill returned the scrap of paper to the plastic desk without meeting Beal's penetrating eyes. He shuffled his feet like a shy child. "I can check again, if you like. But I don't think I'll find anything else."

"You'd better *comb* the entire rabid Hounda infested complex!" Beal shouted. "And don't show your prehistoric face to me again, unless you have discovered the required data, or you are ready to be *severely* punished!"

Bill left, closing the door quietly. He leaned beside a paisley wall dispenser, pulled a handkerchief from it and wiped his forehead. He ran to his yellow desk and thumbed the large, red, General Summons Button on his ratty, blue intercom.

Within three minutes, Bill's dozen weird looking subordinates stood at attention in front of his desk. He stood up, narrowed his eyes and said, "*Timmorey*," as though speaking to intelligent dogs. "Find his records. *Everything*! Even his *bowel function* information! I want it *all*! Half of you, frisk the damned cabinets, the rest of you, squeeze the infernal computers!"

They exchanged looks and each man shrugged in turn. "Sure thing, great and glorious, Bill," one sort of said. "We got nothing better to do, anyway." They spread out in pairs; safety in numbers.

***

Bill sank into his chair-desk and groaned. The twelve helpers patted him on opposite shoulders, jiggling him side to side, then fled for various secluded and safe wings of the complex.

Bill wiped his nose with the sweaty handkerchief. He'd been fortunate the first time he'd been broken to Janitor. But only because he hadn't stayed long enough to be assigned to The Refuse Detail. The Boss of Clean Up had attempted to talk him into that beloved job the moment Bill had unwillingly met him.

***

"I don't desire it!" Bill protested. "I want to *stay* at least *half* alive!"

"It pays more in one *hour* than you get typing for a *day*," the Boss cajoled.

"What's money?" Bill shouted. "I've been ecstatic without it so far! I just want a warm place to sleep and a hunk of meat to chew on!" He backed off a step.

The Boss gestured at the iron doors of the Refuse Room. "It's nice and warm in *there*," he said. "And, you ain't heard nobody *complain* about it, *have you*?"

"No one's *ever* come back *out*!" Bill rasped. "How *could* they *nix* it?" He turned tail.

The Boss caught him by the nape of his neck, and spun him around. "It's an exciting *adventure*!" he said. "It's *unlike* anything you've ever experienced! It's —*unique*!"

"Death always has been a mystery," Bill said, with a sniffle. Then, "How would *you* know what it's like? You've never been further in there than the *first* set of doors!"

The Boss scratched his stubbly chin with dirty fingernails. "That's *beside* the point," he said. "If anything unhappy occurred to you in there, we'd *buy* you a coffin. It's *free*! *We* pay for *everything*!"

"*I* process *all* req forms! Nobody's *ever* bought *even* one *flower* on *your* account, let alone a *casket*, because you can't *bury* a cloud of *vaporized* lackey!" Bill said, sidling toward an Escape Door.

"I got a *fine* idea," the Boss revealed. "I just volunteered *you* for The Refuse Detail, and I even got a sworn, signed statement, penned in your own fine handwriting, it's one of the pleasantest careers imaginable. *Right?*"

Bill could tell the discussion was about to take a depraved turn.

A slender, scared, messenger, wearing an old fashioned black suit, appeared from one of the Service Elevators. With obvious reluctance, he aimed himself toward the men.

The Boss squeezed Bill's arm until it thought about breaking. "Don't you say, *nothing!*" he warned.

The messenger stopped, keeping his distance and warily eyeballing Bill's fine buddy. He coughed, due to several fumes. "Beal wants you *back*," he said.

The messenger's squeaky voice sounded like music to Bill.

"Come with me, *now!*"

That sounded like a symphony to Bill.

The Boss released Bill's arm. "Too bad, pal," he said. Then he grinned. "I got *confidence* in you, though. *You'll* be back. And I'll gamble you'll avidly *wanna* go on Refuse Detail, too!"

Bill jumped into the elevator with the messenger.

"You wouldn't be here if your mother hadn't romanced a Hounda!" Bill shouted, with as much disdain as his fear would allow.

The Boss laughed. "You're just jealous it wasn't *you*," he said, as the elevator doors snapped shut.

***

"Tell Beal that Assistant Director Calooh is here."

Bill blew his nose and thumbed a blue button on his intercom.

"What?" Beal snapped.

"Cal–ooh to see you?–sir?" Bill said. He switched the speaker off, then on.

"...gallbladder!" Beal said darkly. "Show him in. And, don't even try to imagine yourself thinking of leaving! I want to *talk* to you!"

Bill pointed to the correct door and turned his back to his second boss.

Calooh fumbled at the large, ornate door knob with his tiny wing hands without the desired results. He honked with anger and spun around. "Would you kindly *deign* to open this door!" he shouted.

Bill did so, shutting the portal hard after the Pharsey. "Someday," he mumbled, "I'll quit this joint where they hire slope-headed, winged crooks and do something intelligent—stripteasing!" He sat down at his desk and began drafting his resignation—again.

Alderbrian Press

Chapter 3

Grand Canyon Sized Waterloo

It was six in the morning.

Timmorey slipped through the woods. He paused several times at noises but each turned out to be rabbits or squirrels. He increased his pace and twisted through the trees in the straightest path the lush vegetation allowed.

***

A man was squatting by the lake. He had a rifle.

Timmorey drew nearer to him.

"Hi," the man said. He stood up and turned around. "Thought sure you'd been eaten by one of the critters."

Timmorey smiled. "You know none of them around here are big enough to chomp me, and the ones up north that are, would choke to death because I'd go down sideways."

They laughed and sat down on a log.

"Why are you toting iron, today, Alan?"

"I was thinking about some target shooting, maybe,"

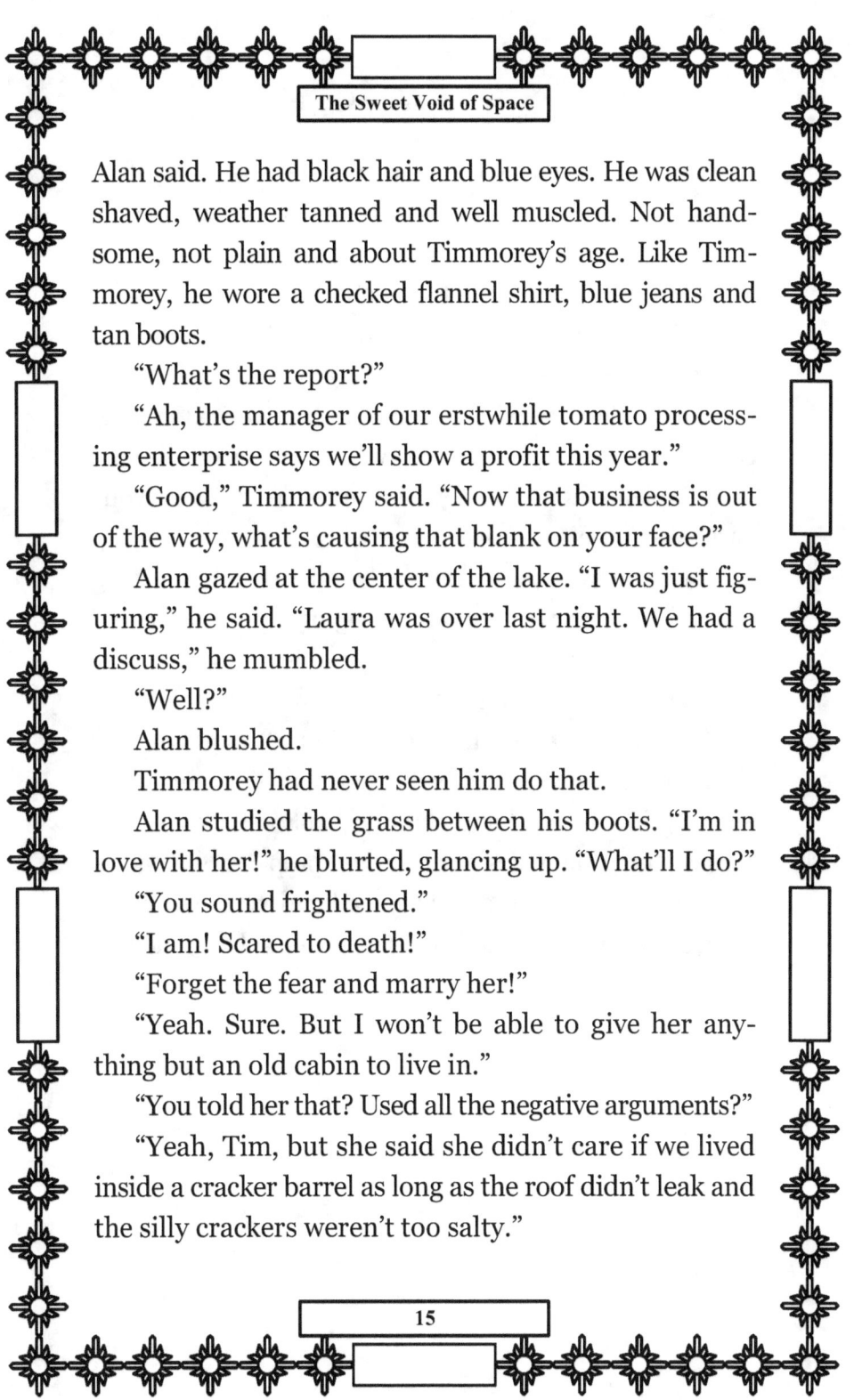

Alan said. He had black hair and blue eyes. He was clean shaved, weather tanned and well muscled. Not handsome, not plain and about Timmorey's age. Like Timmorey, he wore a checked flannel shirt, blue jeans and tan boots.

"What's the report?"

"Ah, the manager of our erstwhile tomato processing enterprise says we'll show a profit this year."

"Good," Timmorey said. "Now that business is out of the way, what's causing that blank on your face?"

Alan gazed at the center of the lake. "I was just figuring," he said. "Laura was over last night. We had a discuss," he mumbled.

"Well?"

Alan blushed.

Timmorey had never seen him do that.

Alan studied the grass between his boots. "I'm in love with her!" he blurted, glancing up. "What'll I do?"

"You sound frightened."

"I am! Scared to death!"

"Forget the fear and marry her!"

"Yeah. Sure. But I won't be able to give her anything but an old cabin to live in."

"You told her that? Used all the negative arguments?"

"Yeah, Tim, but she said she didn't care if we lived inside a cracker barrel as long as the roof didn't leak and the silly crackers weren't too salty."

"So, you thought you'd come out here and kill off all of your fears and negative arguments by target shooting them."

"Don't go playing Mr. Psychiatrist on me," Alan said, "even if you did guess right." He stared at Timmorey. "Help me out!" he finally stammered.

"Okay," Timmorey said. "Marry her. Quick! Please! She came over to fuss at me two nights ago to see if I would plead her case for her or at least twist your ears. Marry her! Quick!"

"Goll darn you, Timmorey! You two go sneaking around behind my back and ganging up on me and *I* expect to hold out! It just ain't possible!"

"What are you gonna do?"

"Marry her," Alan said. He stood up. "I might as well go tell Laura what she already knows. She's planned everything in advanced and she's probably rehearsed what I'll say when she pitilessly makes me propose. She knows me that well." He waved and blended into the trees, mumbling something about a Grand-Canyon-sized Waterloo.

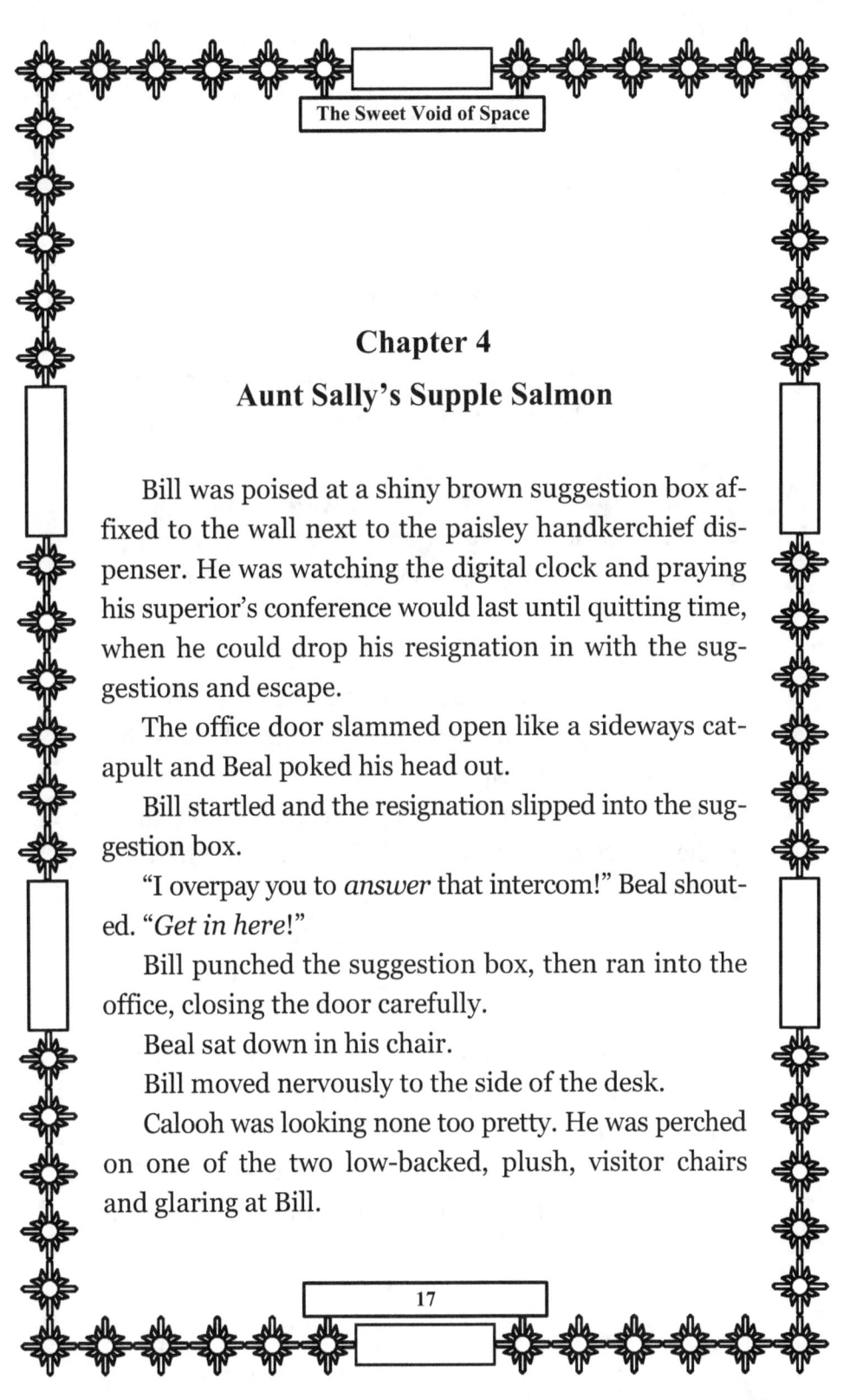

Chapter 4
Aunt Sally's Supple Salmon

Bill was poised at a shiny brown suggestion box affixed to the wall next to the paisley handkerchief dispenser. He was watching the digital clock and praying his superior's conference would last until quitting time, when he could drop his resignation in with the suggestions and escape.

The office door slammed open like a sideways catapult and Beal poked his head out.

Bill startled and the resignation slipped into the suggestion box.

"I overpay you to *answer* that intercom!" Beal shouted. "*Get in here!*"

Bill punched the suggestion box, then ran into the office, closing the door carefully.

Beal sat down in his chair.

Bill moved nervously to the side of the desk.

Calooh was looking none too pretty. He was perched on one of the two low-backed, plush, visitor chairs and glaring at Bill.

Bill smiled nervously.

Calooh snorted.

Bill glanced at the other fat chair on the far side of the desk and wished he was sitting in it. It would provide some sense of security, however false.

Beal shuffled some blue papers, signed the top one, then stared at his secretary. "Where's that information," he demanded.

Bill thought of the iron doors to The Refuse Room, visualizing a cloud of vapor and his perma-metal Identity Plate lying on the perma-cement floor, surrounded by a thundering white fire. He found a voice which he was almost sure wasn't his. "As you thought, sir," he said, "there weren't any other reports on this Timmorey person." He painfully crossed his fingers behind his back. This time, it helped.

Beal looked puzzled, then shrugged and motioned to the empty chair. "Sit down," he said. He lifted the fourth of a paper, giving it another reading.

Bill sat and stole a peep at the Pharsey.

Calooh's eyes were closed and he had changed. He was almost beautiful.

Having suffered his rudeness and his act of contemptuous superiority often, Calooh always retained an air of ugliness to Bill.

Some Pharseys could rub almost any human the wrong way and they often did so simply for the pleasure of it. They were mostly a gang of thieving liars.

The majority of people to whom Bill had spoken felt the same way about the high and mighty flighties, which was a comfort to him.

Beal slammed his bony fist against the desk, smashing a plastic, laser ink eraser flat.

The Pharsey was jarred into hostile re-awareness of his surroundings.

Beal gave Calooh an apologetic look.

It was the first time Beal had acted other than cruel in Bill's presence.

Beal jabbed a finger at Bill. "Timmorey can't get away with *this*!" he shouted. "Just because he was *born* on the planet, he thinks he *owns* it! As if anyone *sane* would *want* to possess *that* hunk of rock and water! And he takes it upon *his* fine self to tell *us*, Operations Central, *we* can't replace *him*, or have a free hand at regaining an *Item*! The audacity! The—" His jaws continued to work, but only hot air escaped.

Bill's eyebrows started to rise, but ceased when he comprehended what Beal was saying. He watched in amazement.

Beal pumped more air from his lungs. Then his face adopted the color of a ripe Earth Tomato.

Beal often became so irate, his face turned red, but this time, it had attained the deepest hue of crimson Bill had ever witnessed.

Beal was visibly sweat-soaking the collar of his jumper suit.

Calooh was so angry, he was hopping, from one clawed foot to the other, on the back of the chair.

This Timmorey must be some *rengel* guy, Bill thought. He's got old Beal stewing and ugly Calooh dancing. I'd like to *meet* this Timmorey, sometime! He could enjoy the antics of his superiors for only a few more moments before he had to suppress a laugh.

Calooh stopped hopping back and forth.

Beal regained his usual dour demeanor. "Listen— What's your name?" he said.

"Bill Wayden," Bill replied, with a secretarial tone. As if you didn't know, he thought.

"Listen, Wayden, you're beaming over to Earth with Calooh. Place this Timmorey under arrest and crackle his disobedient atoms back to me. Do you understand?"

Bill nodded and began biting the fingernails of his left hand. He'd have to retrieve his resignation somehow, and before he left, or Beal would hurl him into The Refuse Room, instead of rewarding him, if he did well on this Timmorey business. He started squirming in his seat.

Calooh was bobbing his head around.

"What's wrong?" Beal asked, his tone diplomatic.

"I was under the assumption that *you* would accompany me! I don't think this man is capable of seizing the situation! Timmorey is a dangerous, forceful man! He has to be handled in a special way. *Surprised, and taken swiftly!*" He started hopping up and down on the back of the chair, with his head still bobbing back and forth.

Bill burst out laughing so hard he nearly slid out of his chair.

"You discourteous, disrespectful, nordhonger!" Beal bellowed, the last word being an incredible obscenity. "You are correct, Calooh, he *is* sorely incapable!" He gestured at Bill. "*Wait* for me at your desk, *nordhonger*!"

Bill staggered out of the room, slamming the door and belly laughing uncontrollably. He slowly sank into his chair and held his aching stomach, resting his swimming head on the desk. He remembered his resignation and sat bolt upright.

Now that he was probably going to be fired and killed, he certainly didn't want anyone, or even any, *thing*, reading the fabulous tear-jerker he had penned. He charged to the Suggestion Box and groaned with frustration. Some crazoid idiot had actually engaged the electro lock, therefore sealing the Box.

He socked the lock with a fist, making something inside the box rattle. Not giving a damn, he kicked the box off the wall and sent it splintering against one of the filing cabinets.

He fished his resignation from the debris. Beside it was a gold-colored can of fish. Aunt Sally's Supple Salmon. This was some worker's method of articulating that something fishy was occurring around Central. He slipped the rectangular can of expensive Earthling delicacies into his hip pocket, shoved the rest of the rubbish behind the filing cabinet, and fed his resignation into the Document Disintegrator wall slot on the far side of Beal's door.

The quitting time bell sounded with more mercy than usual. The dozen odd looking subordinates bolted through the various exits leading to the elevators. Bill vanished out the center set of servo-doors.

Beal stormed from his office.

Calooh followed in his wake, honking furiously.

Chapter 5
The Sweet Void of Space

Bill secured himself into his fifth floor apartment by using the lighted personal Thumb Print Lock. Operations was backwards in most ways but the employees' living quarters were the newest holes with push buttons available on the market.

Anything you wanted was yours for the using. Provided you were ready to scramble in any direction, with no warning, to avoid being clobbered by what you summoned. And if you could locate the correct button for what you desired.

Each apartment had a different floating appliance and furniture pattern. None had a layout showing what should be pressed to get which appliance or piece of furniture or where it would pop up. The Floating System kept the locations changing.

The inner office memo on the Posh Suites, claimed this constant dodging of the appurtenances brought excitement into the lives of the tenants and helped keep them physically fit while preventing boredom after working hours.

It wasn't that way.

Bill had been laid up for a week once when an easy chair (Easily weighing two hundred pounds, according to him.) had smacked him on the forehead and knocked him loony. He still claimed to his friends to have an indentation where the chair had brained him and he usually tried to explain some of his weird stunts by recounting this tragedy.

There was a control panel mounted on the wall beside the door. The portal and the panel never changed position. He punched a button he hoped would bring up a closet and shower. Then he leaped into a corner six feet away.

He was lucky.

The closet sprang up in the center of the room, with the shower stall pressing him against the wall. He wiggled free and slipped his money and identity card into a jumper suit hanging inside the closet. He shoved the can of Aunt Sally's Supple Salmon across the floor and up against the wall beneath the Control Panel.

He undressed and fed his soiled clothing into the slot of the auto cleaning unit attached to the side of the closet. The clothes would be laundered and hung in the closet within five minutes. He hopped into the shower which was already jet pulsing water at the temperature he had pre-programmed.

***

Bill was singing the twenty-third chorus of, The Sweet Void of Space, when someone huge hammered on his door. He chuckled at the increasing thudding, and continued singing.

The door burst off its hinges.

Bill thrust his head between the blue shower curtains and his jaw dropped.

A uniformed Territorial Policeman was framed by the hall light. His shoulders were touching the sides of the doorway. He caressed a Shocker Pistol in one hairy hand and grasped a shiny pair of electronic handcuffs in the other.

Bill tried to stop shaking. "What's going on here?" he demanded, not above a whisper.

The policeman smiled slyly. "You're under arrest!" he stated. "Get dressed and come with me, or you may not be able to walk!"

Bill punched the water-off button and flew from the shower.

The policeman laughed, amused by Bill's fear.

Bill threw on his second jumper. With the help of the officer, he closed what was left of his door by leaning it against the shattered frame.

The policeman clicked one of the cuffs around Bill's left wrist and the other around the special belt buckle of his blue uniform, allowing the short chain to hang loose. "Stick close, jail meat," he said, "and I won't have to burn off your kneecaps!"

"You're kind," Bill said meekly.

The officer yanked the chain and they entered a waiting elevator.

Bill squeezed into a corner and it helped to stop his shaking. A few rumors about the Territorial Police made him less than eager to provoke the power of his guard. He began chewing the nails of one hand and pulling an ear lobe with the other.

The elevator reached ground level with a thud, making Bill feel as if he'd just fallen to the bottom of a towering canyon.

The policeman jerked the chain and they stepped into the sun and onto one of the Walking Belts.

People all around stopped long enough to stare at the poor criminal, before moving on as if nothing were happening.

Bill closed his eyes to avoid those Earth Cow-gazers and shook his head. He couldn't think of anything criminal he had done besides break up the Suggestion Box. Beal wouldn't sick the boppers on him for *that*. No, he'd just dock him a day's pay. He'd done it before. And Beal wouldn't prosecute him for laughing in the crude faces of his supposedly Superior Workers. Why, then, was he being carted away? He started to ask the officer, but, after seeing the mean expression on the man's Earth-Bulldog face, forgot all his questions and decided to play along. Besides, he might be able to sue the policeman, and the Territory, for false arrest. He smiled and gave the bopper a secretive look.

They changed Walking Belts four times, going to the dark center of the planet-wide city to where all the judicial arrangements were struck. They stopped at a towering, black-stone building marked:

SUPERIOR COURT ONE

Bill froze with amazement. I haven't even been *charged* with a crime, he thought, with panic, how can he already be leading me to *trial*? He felt the peevish policeman tugging on the chain and followed the beast through the self-opening metal doors. They slammed shut behind like thunder and he startled, jostling the policeman.

"Another move like *that*, and I get to drill a hole between your *eyes*!" the officer growled. He yanked the chain and half dragged Bill into a round room with a vaulted ceiling.

A semicircular judicial bench crouched like a vicious, ebony animal near the far wall. There were ten chairs, but only four were occupied by judges. Purple hoods revealed their eyes, noses and mouths. Black robes and white gloves concealed all else. They looked decidedly inconsequential compared to the imposing furniture.

Bill noticed the man farthest to his left owned a long, hook nose. The man next to Hooknose, boasted brown, crossed eyes. The two judges on Bill's right seemed almost human.

"Make certain he does not escape, Gran," Hooknose admonished the bopper. "No determining *what* he might try!"

"Whatever *I* attempt," Bill said, with ire, "it won't be a *pre scripted*, *mockery* of a *pseudo-trial*!"

"Shaddap!" the policeman shouted, rattling the chain.

Bill stepped back. "Can—can you tell me what I'm charged with?" he said.

"*We* ask all the questions *here*!" Hooknose snapped. "And, you will not speak until spoken to!" He threw open a folder and shuffled through it until he satisfied his search. He showed a pink paper to his cohorts and they all eyeballed Bill distastefully.

This convinced Bill the two decent appearing members, were not. Especially the man second to his right. He had a distinct sadistic glint in his eyes.

"Are you sure *this* is the man he wants, Studge? It doesn't seem he acts quite right." It was the cross eyed man speaking.

Bill reflected that Hooknoses's name sounded criminal.

"The bird supplied us a holo-picture of him," Studge

said as he peered at the prisoner. "At exactly five thirty today, Beal, Head of Operations Central and the honorable Second in Command, Pharsey Calooh, were attacked from behind in the Ground Car Basement of Operations Central and rendered unconscious by Shocker Ray. Beal was taken away.

"Before he slipped unconscious, Pharsey Calooh swears he witnessed you wielding the weapon and bending over the prone figure of your superior. Pharsey Calooh has charged you with two counts of armed assault and one count of kidnapping.

"How do you plead?"

"*Not guilty*! I was in the *shower* when Beal was crackled senseless! What *motive* could *I* have for kidnapping *my* meal ticket! I want a *fair* jury trial!"

"No matter," Studge said. "I find you guilty as charged and sentence you to eighteen years on Legrun Prison Planet. If you should sagaciously wish to divulge the whereabouts of the honorable Beal, I could lessen the sentence to sixteen years. No?" He waved a hand dismissively.

"This isn't *fair*!" Bill shouted. "I *demand* a jury trial! I *demand* a counselor! You must *honor* my rights to a *public trial*!" Irate, he charged at the bench. The policeman jerked him flat of his back and dragged him along the floor and out the door. He struggled to his feet, enraged. The bopper tugged him around a corner and toward a small iron door with a barred window. Bill yanked the chain with all his strength.

The policeman looked absolutely astounded, lost his balance and fell backwards, striking his head hard against a baseboard.

Bill checked the man's heart, discerned it was still beating, and relief flooded over him. He searched the bopper's pockets until he secured the cuff's little electronic key. He beamed himself free and threw the key angrily into a corner.

He grabbed up the policeman's big shocker gun and ran for the double doors behind him. They hissed open and he charged into the weak sunlight, ignoring the prying eyes of the startled people using the Walking Belts.

He ducked into a tiny alley between the courthouse and a Sub-Police Station. Remembering the shocker pistol, he stopped, stared at it oddly, dropped it to the cobblestones, and fled to an archway. This led to an underground car system.

He raced down the steps and climbed into the first car he saw. He slammed the clear top closed just as the wobbly car began to move, and settled down in the plush plastic seat, breathing hard.

He jerked forward. The lighted display on the plastic dash detailed the ground car's destination as:

Operations Central: P.N. 4422102.

He panicked, slapped the Emergency Stop Button on the dashboard and bolted from the car. Central would be crawling with police. So would the car alley, soon, because he had used the Emergency Stop.

He ran across several dozen tracks and hopped into another idling car. It picked up speed when he sat down and he checked the dash display:

The Temple of Thought: P.N. 22221140.

He wouldn't have to punch the Destination Change Number Buttons as he should have with the first rail car. He breathed a long sigh. Once he reached the Holy Temple, no one could touch him. He could live there for the rest of his marked life. He settled into the plastic-covered cushions, and closed his dry, aching eyes.

Chapter 6
Beal's Bane

Beal regained consciousness. He was lying on his back, strapped to a marble topped table in the middle of a concrete room. Across from his bare feet, was a half open, iron door with a small, wire-mesh window.

He strained his neck and saw he was naked. The straps holding him were transparent, almost to the point of invisibility. He struggled against them, but there wasn't any give.

He inspected the long, tubular light-like fixture affixed to the ceiling. It was lit almost imperceptibly and seemed to be keeping him warm.

A blue Pharsey bounced into the cell, pushing the door wide. Six similar birds followed. They formed two half circles around the table, leaving a corridor leading to the hall.

Beal lifted his head and the first bird placed a hard, smelly pillow under it. He relaxed, watching the doorway.

A white fowl strutted into the room and posed regally at the feet of the prisoner.

"I figured as much, *Calooh*," Beal rumbled. "If *anybody* would go *bad*, it would be *you*! I never could understand the *filthy* politics that greased you into office. Why do *this* at *this* time?"

Calooh hissed. "You know that a Pharsey of the Lofty Preennon Caste cannot bear the humiliation of being a *second* in command, for long," he said, "or to even *remain* in public service without *serving* himself first. It is our *custom*! Even *you* should have guessed my intent when five of the Items fell into *my* Protective Custody. It's sad that you won't join my effort."

"You shouldn't even have to *ask*!" Beal said, livid with rage. "If I were free, I'd tear you and your lackeys to pieces!" He spat at the bird, just falling short of his hated target. "What are your plans for me?"

Calooh cooed. "Do you see that device above you?" he said. "When I leave, it will be turned on full, and you will slowly burn to death. A tan, a rosy sunburn, and worse. Until your ugly flesh is seared from your bones. Every moment, you'll be conscious, and in agony. It should be a most *entertaining* week for you!" He snaked his head closer. "If you had not *degraded* me, even in the *privacy* of your office, your death would be more *merciful*!" he said, hissing with ire. He pompously turned to exit. "Don't you *fret*," he cooed, with mock concern, "those straps are *heat* resistant." He cackled as he left.

The blue Pharseys hopped fearfully after their cruel master and the door clanged shut. The overhead heat fixture flowered into brilliance, illuminating every crack and pockmark in the room. Beal closed his eyes to the glare.

***

After half an hour, to Beal's reckoning, the increase in temperature had him sweating. At this rate, he'd dehydrate and die of thirst *before* he burned to death. He derived *no* comfort from this. He'd have to escape *fast*. When he did, he would stuff a pillow with Calooh's pretty, snowy feathers!

One of the straps was across his diaphragm and elbows, pressing his arms to his sides. The other was across his knees. He began wiggling and squirming against them, blowing out his breath and squeezing himself as thin as possible, pointing his long toes forward and back, prising against the marble table top with his heels and fingers. He smiled grimly. They hadn't bothered to place self--adjusting restraints around him. He *could* slip free.

Eventually.

Chapter 7

Nothing Runs Funnier

"I don't think you should worry so, Alan," Laura said. She looked stylish in her yellow blouse, slacks and shoes. "Timmorey was raised in the woods, same as you. He won't fall into any big holes and get bent." She settled next to him on his brown sofa.

"Yeah, I know," Alan said. "I just can't figure what should take him so long." He rubbed the nape of his neck with his big hand. "Why don't *you* brew some coffee, while *I* fret?"

Laura smiled and winked one of her pretty, pale-blue eyes. "Okay, but don't worry yourself away." She went to a cabinet above Alan's new, double-bowl sink, to take down his old, battered, tin coffee pot.

***

Timmorey tightened a last screw and stood back to study his handiwork. It had taken a lot of thought and experimentation, a few funny mistakes and all his spare technical components, but he had accomplished his goal.

There was a tiny, gleaming, circular addition on the

two side walls of the Teleportation Chamber, at about waist height. These devices looked similar to blue, electric eyes, but were actually micro-miniaturized Teleporters.

If someone attempted to crackle to Earth via his porter now, without his best regards, they would be zapped back to whence they had originated. And within a split second after breaking the thin, invisible, Secondary Teleporter Beams.

He chuckled. If old feathers arrives while I'm calling on Alan and Laura, he thought, that foul fowl will probably, mercifully, swear himself to death over this.

He put the screwdriver away by tossing it into the root cellar, closed the trapdoor, straightened the bear rug over it, caught up his shotgun, and exited the cabin, locking it up.

He read the stars through a break in the trees, realized he was later than he'd thought, cut around the cabin, crossed a clearing he often used as a garden, and entered the woods. He met a brook and followed it for about three hundred yards until he found a well worn path. At the end of this, stood Alan's cabin. It was neater in outside appearance than Timmorey's, mainly due to Laura, who had been planing, for a very long time, to move in. Alan bucked every change she made, so, many compromises were negotiated. He knocked on the factory made door. This was one of Laura's victories.

Alan's face showed in the light. "Come on in!" he said. "I thought a possum had gobbled you!" He closed the door and shoved an old hickory chair at Timmorey. This was one of Alan's dubious triumphs. "Sit and repose your—ears." He noted the shotgun. "What's with you carrying that?" he said.

Laura raised her eyebrows.

"I caught wind of some poachers trespassing all over my north-side lake property," Timmorey said, speaking only half truthfully. "Thought I'd give them a scare. That's why I'm so late. Probably try again going home —the long way."

"Hate to say it," Alan said, "but we'll have to put up fences, yet, to keep them away. Scare 'em good, if you get the chance. I'll help, if you need it. Nothing runs funnier than a surprised poacher!"

They all laughed.

Laura handed each of them a cup of coffee, poured herself one and sat on the couch beside Alan. She sipped at the steaming brew. "I hear you unmercifully *beat* Alan into proposing to me," she said. "*I* had the same general thought but waited to see how *you* would help me. Besides, I didn't want to seem *too* unladylike."

Alan grabbed a handful of her blond hair and shook her head tenderly. "She mumbled the proposal right along with me, just like I predicted," he said. "She even helped me once when I got stuck."

Timmorey smiled. He laid the gun beside his chair, drank some coffee and stared into the crackling fire in the hearth to his left. "Will either of you be venturing into town tomorrow?" he said.

"Yeah. Laura and I thought we'd go in, in the morning, to buy some frills she can't possibly live without. You wanna come?" Alan said. He noticed Timmorey's far away, troubled expression, and sighed.

"Ahh—no," Timmorey said. "I have something else I must do tomorrow. It's pressing."

Laura set her cup on a table beside the sofa. "What is it you want from town?" she asked.

Timmorey fished in his shirt pocket, then handed her a paper. "I've got it written here," he said. "Put it all on credit for me." He downed the rest of his coffee.

Laura unfolded the long list and she and Alan looked bemused. "This looks like electrical components," Laura said. "Err—you really *need* this stuff?"

Timmorey smiled. "Yes," he said. "I'm trying to build something. And don't *gape* at me, Alan. Everybody has a secret hobby."

"I didn't *say* anything," Alan protested. "I just can't figure out what you're going to do with a bunch of wires besides make a color coded clothes hanger. Or, maybe, an electric critter trap."

Timmorey turned to him as if he had guessed correctly. "Just may be," he said. He reconsidered. "You'd probably get caught up inside it, before the poor critters had a chance, and break it beyond any hope of repair. That's how *you'd* labor to *kill* a critter!"

"Who was it taught *you* how to *shoot*?" Alan retorted.

"His father," Laura piped in. "His father taught *you* to shoot. Come to think of it, he taught *me* how, too."

"Seems he taught everybody around how to shoot," Alan said. He elbowed Laura. "He didn't do such a good job on this subject. She can't hit even a stuffed stump!" Laura socked him in the stomach. He doubled over, laughing.

"He taught her a *mean* right hook, though," Timmorey said. Laura swung at him playfully. He ducked.

Alan caught her and put his empty cup in her hand. "Go put this away, *please*," he said, giving her a gentle shove.

"It's getting late," Timmorey said.

"Yeah," Alan said. "I'd better get Laura home. It's past her bedtime. If she doesn't get her sleep, she won't want to get up for town tomorrow 'till noon!"

Laura stamped her size seven foot. "You didn't ask *me* if I was ready to return home, or even sleepy!" she said.

"Are you ready to return home, my dear?" Alan asked,

with exaggerated politeness.

"No!"

"Let's get started then," Timmorey said. He hefted his shotgun and entered the night.

"I'm not going!" Laura stated. Alan started without her. She followed, closing the cabin door and laughing.

They walked a path worn by Laura's and Alan's constant comings and goings. This led to a dirt road beside the woods.

Chapter 8

The Temple of Thought

Bill startled awake.

"Pay me, mister!" his tinny sounding ground car insisted. "I have completed all the sad, demeaning services required of me by law! Pay me! *Now*!"

Bill calmed down, read the fare on the lighted display, thumbed coins into the slot next to it, and struggled out of the snotty, cramped car.

To his dismay, he was still several yards from the front of the Temple of Thought; a huge, white edifice which almost resembled an Earth Greek amphitheater. There were armed police, three deep, surrounding it. He could tell they were ready to shoot on sight; their holster flaps were unfastened.

He backed into the ground car alley and peeked around the corner of the book shop next to him. He studied the policemen. His stomach jumped. One was the bopper from whom he had escaped. The officer was holding his helmet in the crook of his left elbow. He had an analgesic bandage on the back of his head

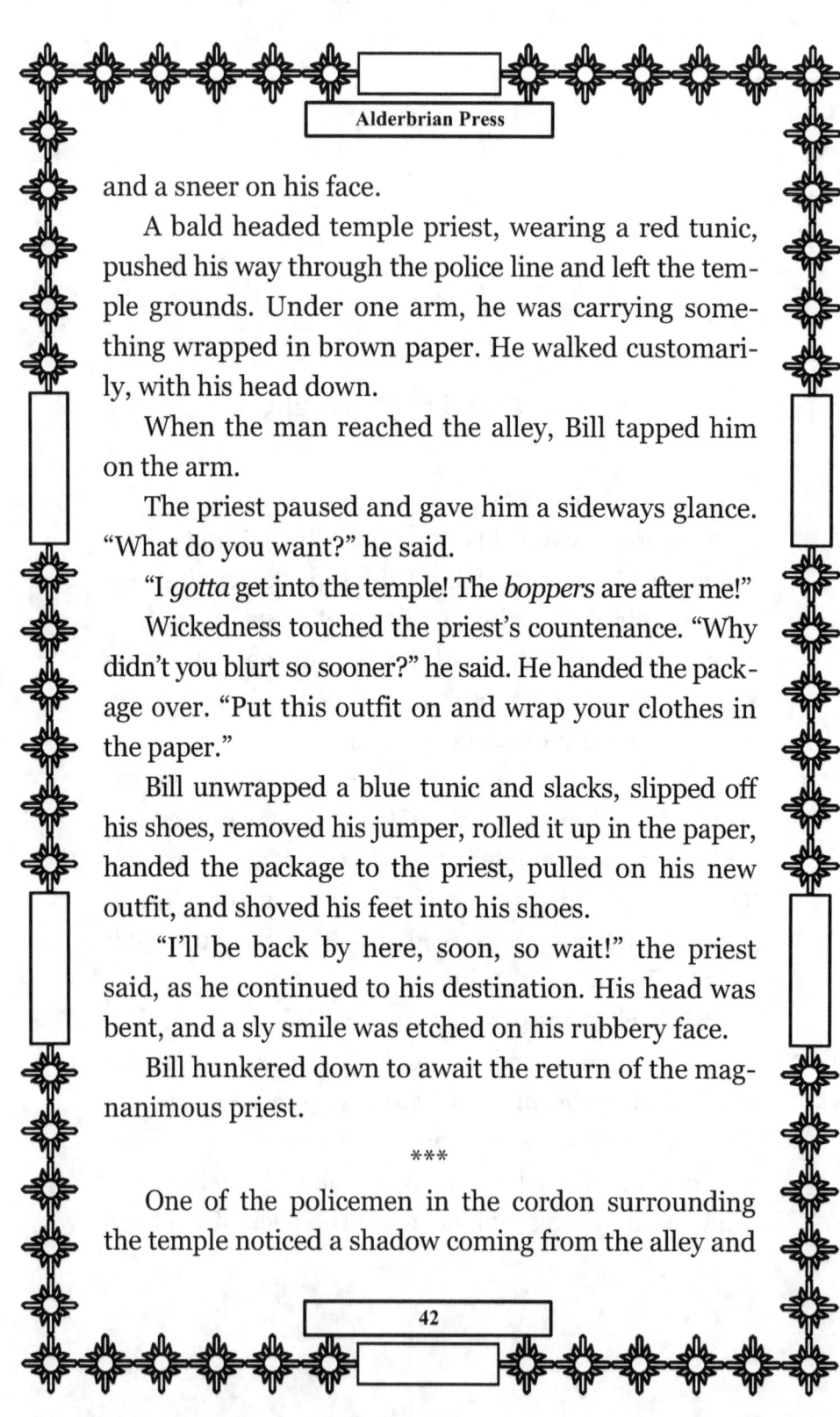

and a sneer on his face.

A bald headed temple priest, wearing a red tunic, pushed his way through the police line and left the temple grounds. Under one arm, he was carrying something wrapped in brown paper. He walked customarily, with his head down.

When the man reached the alley, Bill tapped him on the arm.

The priest paused and gave him a sideways glance. "What do you want?" he said.

"I *gotta* get into the temple! The *boppers* are after me!"

Wickedness touched the priest's countenance. "Why didn't you blurt so sooner?" he said. He handed the package over. "Put this outfit on and wrap your clothes in the paper."

Bill unwrapped a blue tunic and slacks, slipped off his shoes, removed his jumper, rolled it up in the paper, handed the package to the priest, pulled on his new outfit, and shoved his feet into his shoes.

"I'll be back by here, soon, so wait!" the priest said, as he continued to his destination. His head was bent, and a sly smile was etched on his rubbery face.

Bill hunkered down to await the return of the magnanimous priest.

***

One of the policemen in the cordon surrounding the temple noticed a shadow coming from the alley and investigated. When he saw the color of the tunic, he startled, then he blinked at Bill's mop of hair. "You must be one of the new novices they warned us about," he said.

Bill was too terrified to answer.

"You having some kind of vision 'er something?" the bopper asked.

Bill half nodded and grabbed himself by the throat. He rolled his eyes in opposite directions and flopped flat of his chest.

The bopper ran to the cordon and summoned a couple of his bored buddies. Holding him warily by an odd arm or leg, they carried Bill, face down, into the temple, and laid him on the cool, rock floor.

Several lesser temple attendants, in long orange tunics, wandered over, staring stupidly.

Bill religiously remained on his stomach in case the bopper he escaped noticed the commotion and ventured over to investigate. He also lay very still, holding his breath and praying.

The policeman who discovered Bill, turned to one of the puzzled attendants. "He was squatt'n in a ground car alley, eyeball'n the cobblestones, when he went into the crazies. I figured I should bring him in here. It *is* one of yours?"

The brainy attendant suffered cognition lock.

"Be very solicitous!" the Dalph, or director of the

temple, who was wearing a red tunic, warned from behind the group. He dropped to one knee beside Bill and gazed at the policemen in a fair imitation of reverence. "This man is holy," he said softly. "You should bow down before him! He has received divine inspiration on this strange but auspicious day, and you have been privileged to witness it!" He signaled two attendants in orange tunics. "Take him to the Pilgrim Contemplation Room, my brothers, and make him somewhat comfortable."

The acolytes hustled Bill away so fleetly it was conceivable this was not the first such request they had received from their sly leader.

The three boppers made small circle signs in the air with their thumbs and respectfully lowered their helmeted heads.

The Dalph nodded. "You have performed correctly in bringing our hairy holy one to us, my brothers," he told them. "Divine grace shall glisten upon you."

They filed solemnly out of the temple and began bragging up and down the ranks how they had just been saved and, possibly, purified.

The Dalph strode across the echoing central chamber to the left wall. He strutted through a curtain of red, soundproof beads, into a tiny, darkened room.

There was a shabby cot in the far corner. Bill was laying there. He leaped up and shook the Dalph's hand.

"Thanks a *hispic!*" he said. "I thought I was *fried* for!" He wiped his forehead with the back of his hand.

"Glad to be of service," the Dalph mumbled humbly.

"It was almost like you were *looking* for me, the way you came by with this suit."

"I wasn't. I was taking it to be deloused."

Bill kicked his shoes off, divested himself of the tunic and slacks, threw them on the floor, snatched up his shoes, and backed against the wall. "Why didn't you *tell* me *sooner?*" he demanded, with disgust, starting to scratch everywhere he could reach.

The Dalph laughed. "I'm afraid we've got a sticky situation here," he said. "And I don't mean delousing *you.*" He perched on the cot. "I just declared you to be holy and blessed with odd visions. Unless you invent a way of leaving which is acceptable to my flock, you're going to have to make fiery speeches and be worshiped three times a day, for the rest of your godly life."

Bill considered this as he scratched. It didn't sound half bad. At least he'd have three free meals every day and a place to sleep. But pretending to be holy, when he wasn't, was another weird twingo, altogether.

In the strictest sense, he wasn't religious. He didn't go to any one church, temple or shrine, but he was a near believer. He believed in worshiping in his own way, living a quiet life and taking a shower now and then.

He slapped his nape, doing in the only louse he'd

found and cocked his head at the Dalph.

"Why not tell them I died during the night of vision exhaustion and my body was taken to a secret burial ground for a sacred rite," he said. "You *cog* they'll swallow *that*?"

The Dalph shrugged. "Who knows. We'll try it and see. We'll have to fix you so you won't be recognized." He placed his elbow on his knee and his chin on his palm. "Inspiration strikes!" he said. "Wait here!"

***

The Dalph returned with an inferior false beard and mustache. He stuck them on Bill, making him resemble a top-heavy hedge, and stood back, judging. He appeared doubtful, then enthusiastic.

"What now?" Bill asked, suspiciously.

"You'll be a silent, nudist, pilgrim visiting me to learn more about our religion." He engaged Bill in a head lock before the poor man could react. "We'll have to shave you bald, though, to fit the part. Nobody'll recognize you, *then*!"

Despite Bill's howls of protestation, the Dalph pulled a portable shaver from his slacks pocket and wildly started clipping.

***

When he was released, Bill was bald and naked, except for the fake whiskers, and his socks and shoes.

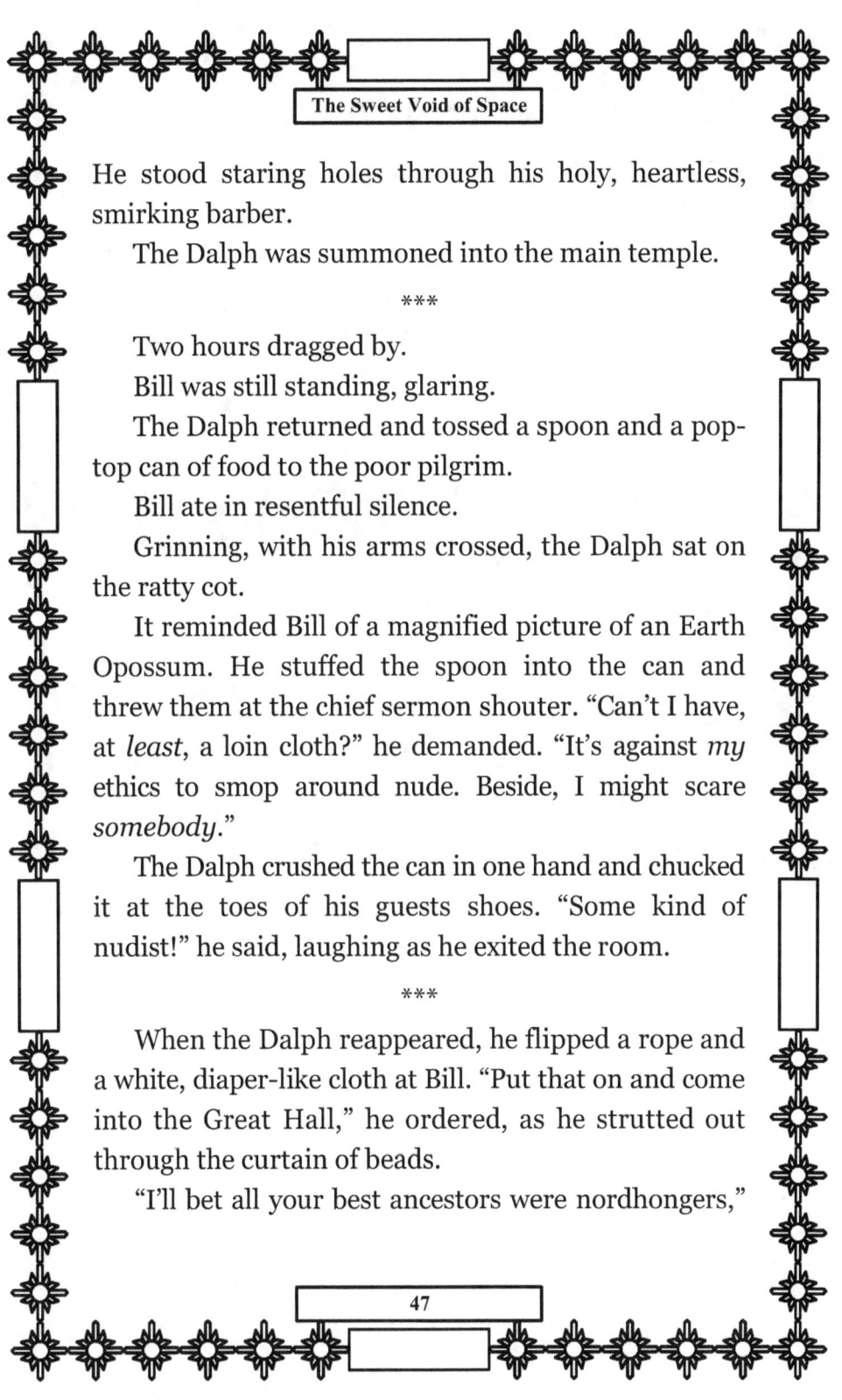

He stood staring holes through his holy, heartless, smirking barber.

The Dalph was summoned into the main temple.

***

Two hours dragged by.

Bill was still standing, glaring.

The Dalph returned and tossed a spoon and a pop-top can of food to the poor pilgrim.

Bill ate in resentful silence.

Grinning, with his arms crossed, the Dalph sat on the ratty cot.

It reminded Bill of a magnified picture of an Earth Opossum. He stuffed the spoon into the can and threw them at the chief sermon shouter. "Can't I have, at *least*, a loin cloth?" he demanded. "It's against *my* ethics to smop around nude. Beside, I might scare *somebody*."

The Dalph crushed the can in one hand and chucked it at the toes of his guests shoes. "Some kind of nudist!" he said, laughing as he exited the room.

***

When the Dalph reappeared, he flipped a rope and a white, diaper-like cloth at Bill. "Put that on and come into the Great Hall," he ordered, as he strutted out through the curtain of beads.

"I'll bet all your best ancestors were nordhongers,"

Bill muttered. He tied the diaper securely and stepped timidly into the noisy crowd gathering for the evening services. He felt his sense of balance performing weird tricks, his head spun, the lighting shifted, and his stomach felt as though it were falling out of his body.

Chapter 9

That Smoothed Down Stump

Timmorey trooped into his cabin, leaving the door wide open and laid the shotgun across the footstool within easy reach.

He went to the sink and filled a pan with well water. He set the pan onto an eye of the bottle gas grill to boil.

There was a thud against one of the inner walls of the Teleportation Chamber. Someone grunted, "Nordhonger!" and fell down.

Timmorey grabbed up his shotgun, pressed his thumb against the Print Sensor embedded in the knob of the door, to unlock it, and opened the porter. He nearly did a double take when he saw a bald man on his knees, wearing what appeared to be fake face hair, a diaper, socks, and shoes.

Bill struggled to his feet and took a dazed step forward.

"Hold it!" Timmorey said.

Bill saw the bygone weapon aimed at him and gulped

with fear. He put both hands on top of his aching head and looked up with effort. "Where am I?"

"Earth."

"You Timmorey?"

Timmorey lowered the shotgun and nodded.

"Then, I wanna talk to you about this *bird*," Bill said. He started forward, then teetered weakly.

Timmorey shut off the auto return beams by tapping the barrel of the shotgun against a toggle control on the outside, right wall of the chamber. He caught Bill in one arm just before Bill's face could become acquainted with the floor. He leaned the gun against the porter door, carried Bill to the cot and laid him out on his back.

Bill groaned and opened his eyes.

"You hold off talking while I take care of that—don't know what it is you have—a cut bump or a bumpy cut," Timmorey said. He soaked a clean rag in the pan of water on the bottle gas grill and began washing the small amount of blood from the wound.

Bill closed his eyes and was snoring in seconds.

***

When Bill awoke, he found himself wearing a pair of faded blue jeans and a checked flannel shirt which was too large. He sat up. The effort was answered by a pang in his head.

Timmorey was making adjustments to a part of

the teleporter.

Bill stood up slowly and watched. "What are you doing?" he asked.

Timmorey tightened a new screw and straightened up. He flipped the screwdriver into the open root cellar. "Just widening the Automatic Return Beam on my doorway," he said. He poured steaming tea into cups and tendered one to his guest. "What bird did you mean?" he said, as he sat down on the stool.

Bill took the cot. He touched the top of his head with gentle fingers. "The bird's *Calooh*," he said. "He's Second in Command at Operations Central. I guess you know that. He's got some grudge against you. You'd know that, too. Well, he and Beal, the big boss of Operations, were leaving Central to come here, I guess, to do something about you, when they were attacked and Beal was whackowed—er—kidnapped. I was blamed by that crooked, foul, fowl, and the law is after me. Only thing that really bothers me is, who would *want* Beal, even to kill him?" He slurped his tea.

"Calooh, for power," Timmorey said. "What do *you* plan to do about the matter?"

"I don't know," Bill mumbled. "I don't even know, for sure, how I got the dubious thrill of being *here*."

"What are you at Operations?" Timmorey asked.

"Beal's Administrative Secretary," Bill said.

Timmorey appeared as if he recalled something

that should have been obvious to him.

Bill shook his head and looked surprised.

"What?" Timmorey asked.

"It doesn't hurt anymore!"

"Herbs in the tea," Timmorey said.

Bill sighed sadly. "I'm facing eighteen years on Leg-run Prison Planet, without a hint of parole. You have any ideas?" he asked.

"Yes," Timmorey said, "we're going hunting. You ever used an Earth rifle where you hail from?" He knelt, reached into the root cellar and brought up two packs of cartridges. One box for rifle, the other for shotgun. He tossed the first at his visitor and opened the second.

Bill caught the box and stuffed it into his shirt pocket. "A simulated one at a side show," he said. "But, what about Calooh and *Beal*?"

"Plenty of time to deal with that," Timmorey said. He reached into the cellar, lifted out an ammo belt, filled it with shotgun shells and buckled it around his waist. He closed the trapdoor and covered it with the rug. He picked up the gun, shut the porter door, sealed it with his thumb print, and stepped outside. "Come on," he said.

Bill was reluctant to leave the comfort and safety of the cabin, but did.

Timmorey locked the door with an old fashioned key. The lock and key appeared vintage but were state of the art reproductions embedded with electronic security sensors.

Bill stared at the chirping birds and the squirrels frisking in the woods. "I don't see much nature around Central," he said. "I shoot in a room where a projectionist shows you holo-pictures that *look* like animals. I don't know if I can kill a *real* one!"

"If we find what *I'm* after," Timmorey said, "just fire high over their heads. That should be fine." He went around the cabin and down the path leading to the brook.

Bill tagged along reluctantly.

***

They reached Alan's cabin as he and Laura were leaving for town.

"You decide to come along?" Alan asked.

"Nope," Timmorey said, "just want to borrow that extra rifle of yours. *If* you haven't *thrown* it away." He winked at Laura.

"You *know* better than that, Tim," Alan said. "And, that flirting will have to stop *after* Laura and I are married." He rummaged loudly in the cabin and returned with the rifle. "Why do you want it, and who's your shiny headed friend?"

Bill received the weapon, pulled the box from his pocket and stuffed shells into the loading chamber.

"This is the weird cousin I told you about once," Tim-

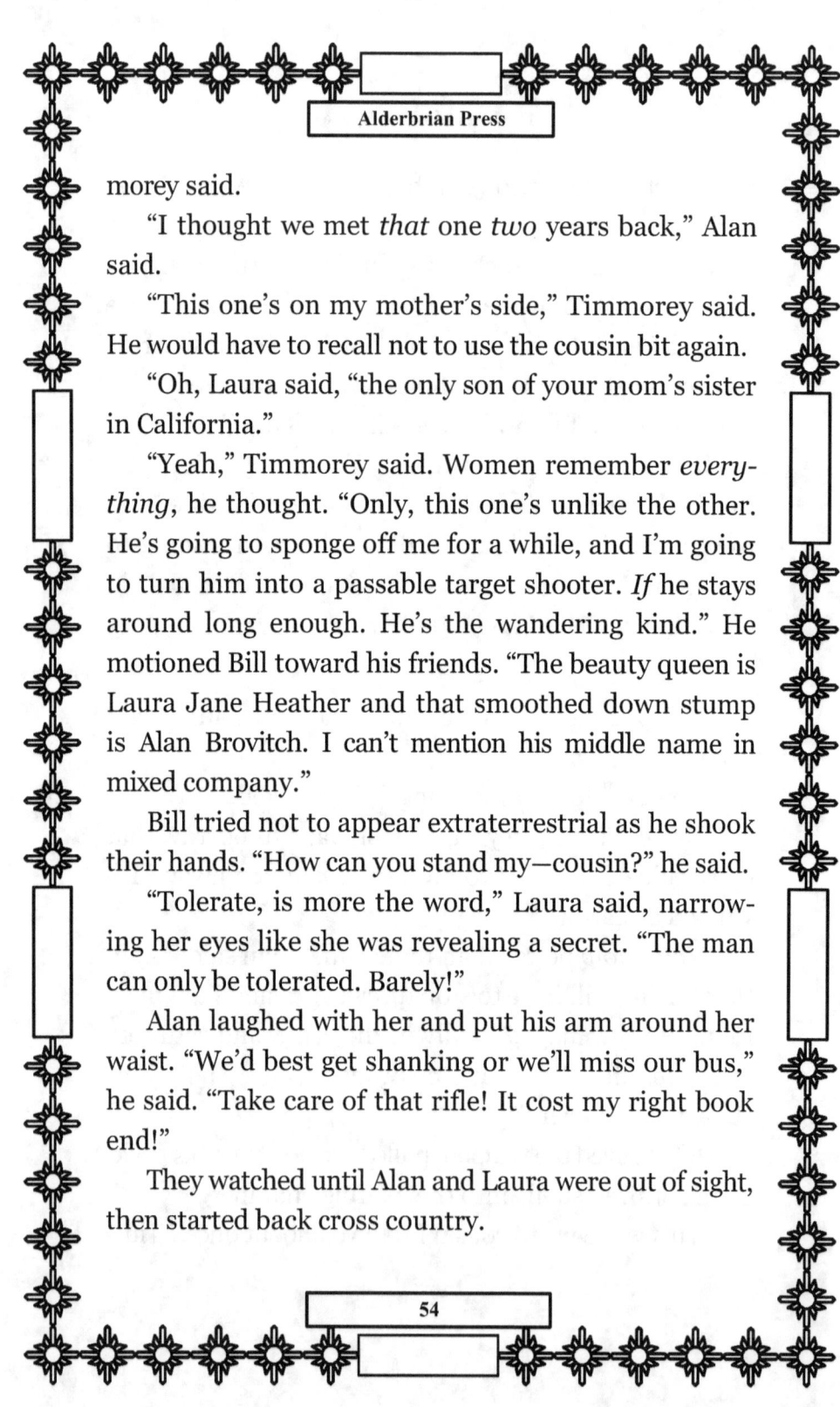

morey said.

"I thought we met *that* one *two* years back," Alan said.

"This one's on my mother's side," Timmorey said. He would have to recall not to use the cousin bit again.

"Oh, Laura said, "the only son of your mom's sister in California."

"Yeah," Timmorey said. Women remember *everything*, he thought. "Only, this one's unlike the other. He's going to sponge off me for a while, and I'm going to turn him into a passable target shooter. *If* he stays around long enough. He's the wandering kind." He motioned Bill toward his friends. "The beauty queen is Laura Jane Heather and that smoothed down stump is Alan Brovitch. I can't mention his middle name in mixed company."

Bill tried not to appear extraterrestrial as he shook their hands. "How can you stand my—cousin?" he said.

"Tolerate, is more the word," Laura said, narrowing her eyes like she was revealing a secret. "The man can only be tolerated. Barely!"

Alan laughed with her and put his arm around her waist. "We'd best get shanking or we'll miss our bus," he said. "Take care of that rifle! It cost my right book end!"

They watched until Alan and Laura were out of sight, then started back cross country.

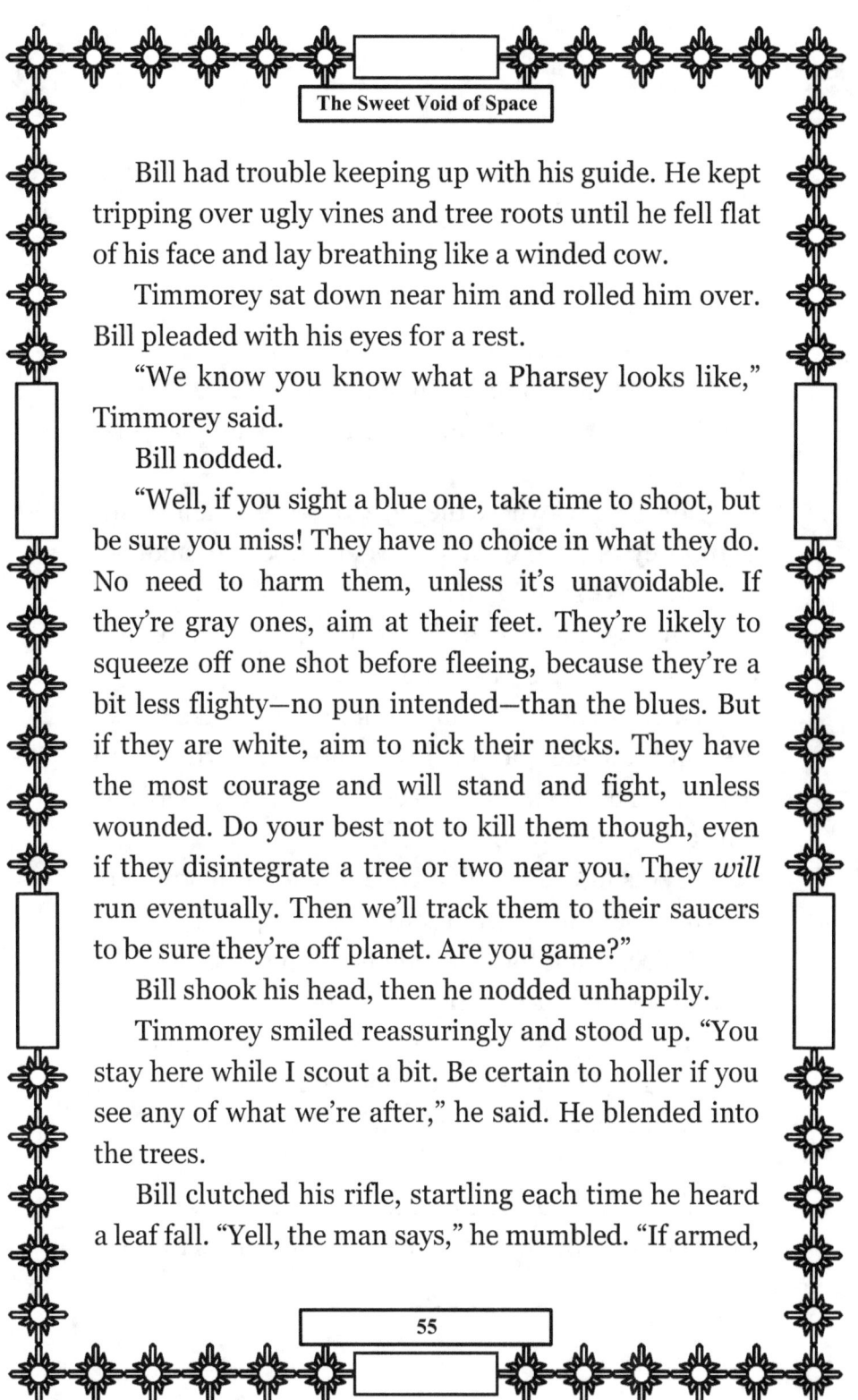

Bill had trouble keeping up with his guide. He kept tripping over ugly vines and tree roots until he fell flat of his face and lay breathing like a winded cow.

Timmorey sat down near him and rolled him over. Bill pleaded with his eyes for a rest.

"We know you know what a Pharsey looks like," Timmorey said.

Bill nodded.

"Well, if you sight a blue one, take time to shoot, but be sure you miss! They have no choice in what they do. No need to harm them, unless it's unavoidable. If they're gray ones, aim at their feet. They're likely to squeeze off one shot before fleeing, because they're a bit less flighty—no pun intended—than the blues. But if they are white, aim to nick their necks. They have the most courage and will stand and fight, unless wounded. Do your best not to kill them though, even if they disintegrate a tree or two near you. They *will* run eventually. Then we'll track them to their saucers to be sure they're off planet. Are you game?"

Bill shook his head, then he nodded unhappily.

Timmorey smiled reassuringly and stood up. "You stay here while I scout a bit. Be certain to holler if you see any of what we're after," he said. He blended into the trees.

Bill clutched his rifle, startling each time he heard a leaf fall. "Yell, the man says," he mumbled. "If armed,

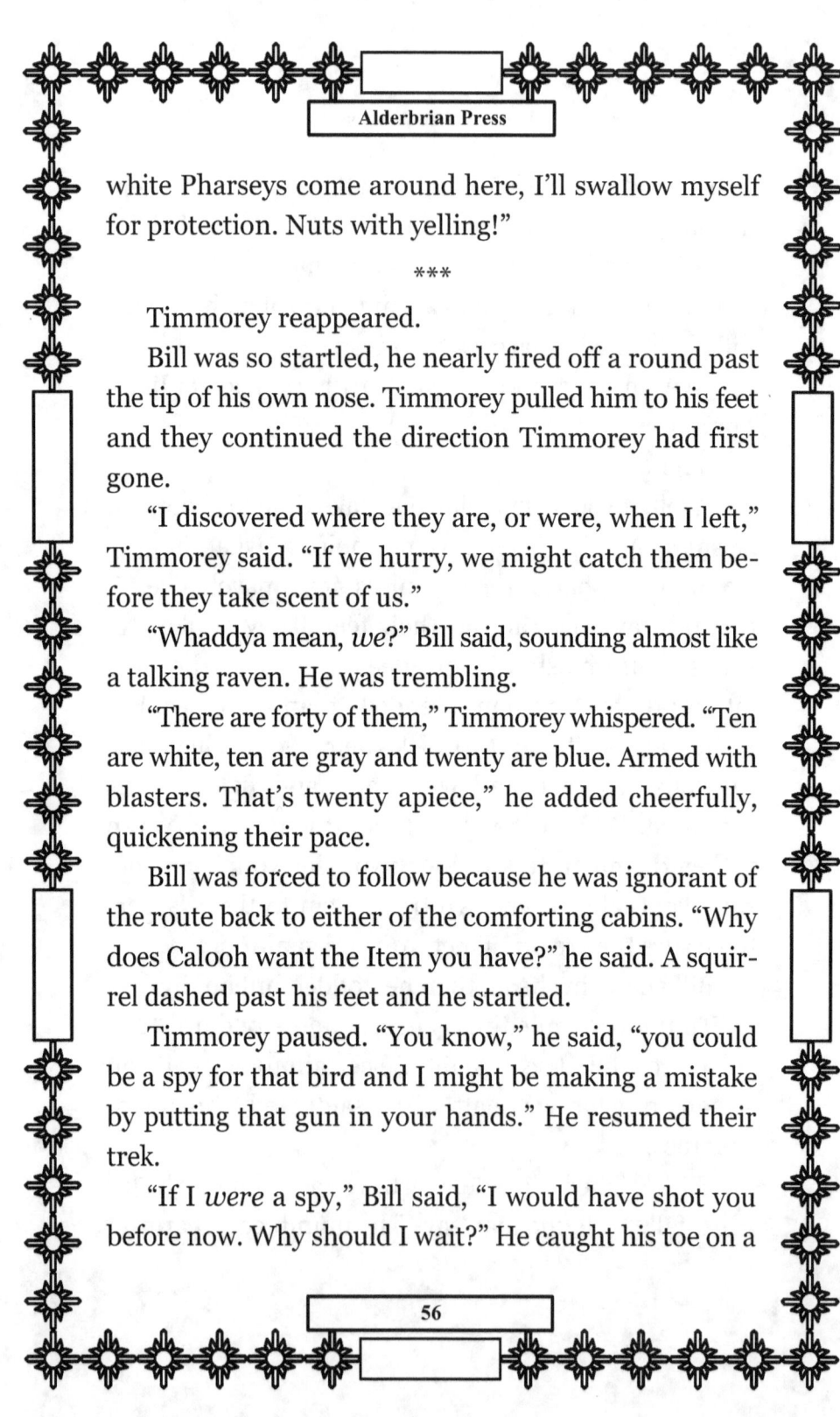

white Pharseys come around here, I'll swallow myself for protection. Nuts with yelling!"

***

Timmorey reappeared.

Bill was so startled, he nearly fired off a round past the tip of his own nose. Timmorey pulled him to his feet and they continued the direction Timmorey had first gone.

"I discovered where they are, or were, when I left," Timmorey said. "If we hurry, we might catch them before they take scent of us."

"Whaddya mean, *we*?" Bill said, sounding almost like a talking raven. He was trembling.

"There are forty of them," Timmorey whispered. "Ten are white, ten are gray and twenty are blue. Armed with blasters. That's twenty apiece," he added cheerfully, quickening their pace.

Bill was forced to follow because he was ignorant of the route back to either of the comforting cabins. "Why does Calooh want the Item you have?" he said. A squirrel dashed past his feet and he startled.

Timmorey paused. "You know," he said, "you could be a spy for that bird and I might be making a mistake by putting that gun in your hands." He resumed their trek.

"If I *were* a spy," Bill said, "I would have shot you before now. Why should I wait?" He caught his toe on a vine and stumbled.

Timmorey saved him from falling. "To worm the location of the Item from me," he said. He pushed a branch aside and let it go after he passed the sapling.

The branch struck Bill on the side of the neck. He rubbed the spot and glared at the back of Timmorey's head. "If *I* were a spy, he said, "*I* would have shot you for *that*! Item, or no!"

Timmorey stopped. "You're not a spy, and I know it," he said. "A Pharsey of Calooh's ilk places a special, sensor controlled, wire collar around their spies' necks. If they displease, fail or betray their masters, the collar tightens and, pop, goes their head. It's on all his blue Pharseys and some of his grays."

Bill fingered his throat and swallowed uneasily. "Yeah, but what about the reasons for—"

Timmorey gestured.

Bill fell silent.

"I'll tell you about that later, *if* you'll be effective for me *now*. We'd better get quiet before it's too late to take those Pharseys unaware," he said. He broke into a fast trot.

Bill came swearing after, tripping, staggering and bumping into weird bushes and scary trees.

After a few minutes of this, Timmorey put his free hand out behind himself, slowed Bill to a walk, then drew him close. "Remember," he said, "they're *blaster* armed, so move as quietly as possible. Not a sound, mind you, or you won't be able to tell your cute, but no doubt goofy, grandchildren about this!"

Bill rubbed his throat. "If you keep grabbing me like *that*," he complained, "I won't be able to *see* straight."

"Sorry," Timmorey said. "Now, be calm and get ready. If they're still there, as soon as we top this rise, the white Pharseys will rush us, the blues will turn tail—still no pun intended—and the grays will hide behind trees, or the white Pharseys.

"In other words, ignore everything blue. Be certain you miss close what you're shooting at, and that you don't hit me, or yourself! If you loose the rifle, run like the wind, in any direction. I'll find you later."

Shaking almost audibly, Bill swallowed the dry knot in his throat and grasped the rifle thankfully tighter with both hands.

They charged, side by side, over the rise.

In the clearing, a fat rabbit sat chewing on some cabbage. It gazed at them, then returned to its feast.

Timmorey shrugged. "We'll have to read their tracks and see where they headed," he said.

Untrained in such skills, Bill sat on the grass and witnessed.

The rabbit gave up its cabbage leaf and hopped around beside Timmorey, sniffing the grass wherever he placed a hand. He petted the jack behind the ears and said something to it. The rabbit raised on its haunches, sampled the air, then skittered across the clearing to an old tree trunk and went into a point. Timmorey spoke to the jack again, patted it on the back, and motioned for Bill to join them. The rabbit considered Bill, then returned to the more interesting cabbage leaf.

Timmorey pointed the direction the rabbit had. "According to Mr. Rabbit," he said, "the stinky Pharseys went that a way. Around the north shore of the lake."

Bill scratched his scalp, avoiding the cut. "You expect me to believe you talked to that, whatever it is?" he asked.

"The rabbit does," Timmorey said. "Besides, you yak at Pharseys every day, don't you?"

Bill mulled this over.

Sensing the conversation was about it, the jack hopped to Bill's feet. He knelt, lifted its chin with a finger and looked into its eyes. "I apologize," he mumbled. The rabbit licked his thumb, then revisited its green meal. Bill stood up. "Now what?" he said.

"We go a track'n again," Timmorey said cheerfully, "That way! And we don't stop until we make sure they haven't circled the lake to my cabin, or until we get off at least one good shot over the heads of those flighty, feathery, brothers, and chase them off planet!"

Chapter 10
Janitor Fever

Beal slipped down until his arms were free of the first restraint. After bringing his head from under it, he sat up and pulled his legs from beneath the second strap. He slid off the table and staggered out of the direct rays of the heat lamp. He sank to the floor, leaned back against the cool wall, and inspected his slightly burned body. It was painful to move, but getting out of his cell would be worth the price.

He stood up and went to the iron door. He hooked his fingers through the holes of the wire mesh window and pulled hard. The door latch clicked and settled into a more secure closure. "Damn!" he said.

He smashed his fist against the mesh, causing the material to buckle outward. He hit the window again, ignoring the pain at each blow until a top corner of the mesh tore loose. He bent this down and pulled the mesh toward him, ripping it slowly away from the square frame until he could get his arm through.

After experimenting with the odd, hoop-shaped latch,

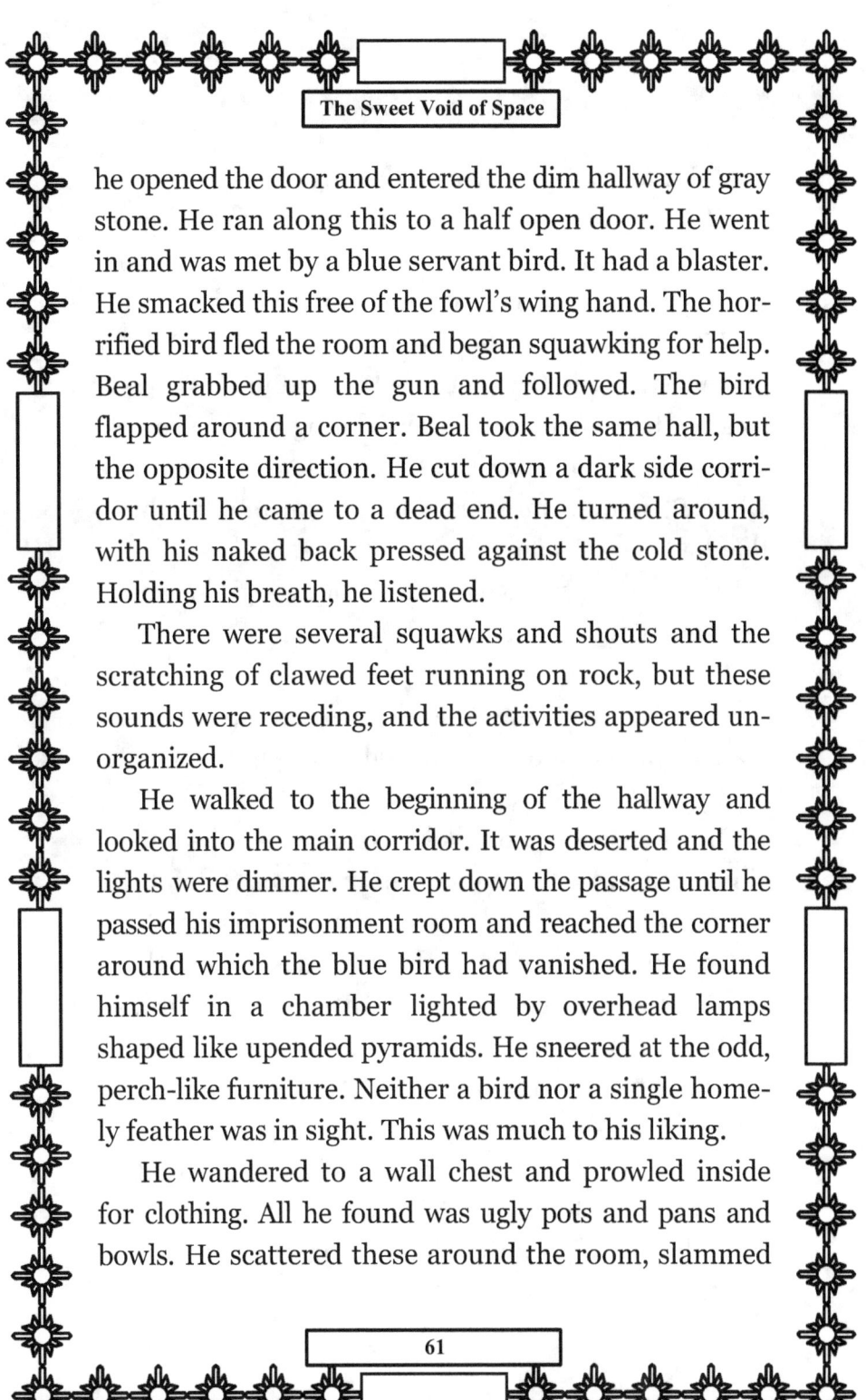

he opened the door and entered the dim hallway of gray stone. He ran along this to a half open door. He went in and was met by a blue servant bird. It had a blaster. He smacked this free of the fowl's wing hand. The horrified bird fled the room and began squawking for help. Beal grabbed up the gun and followed. The bird flapped around a corner. Beal took the same hall, but the opposite direction. He cut down a dark side corridor until he came to a dead end. He turned around, with his naked back pressed against the cold stone. Holding his breath, he listened.

There were several squawks and shouts and the scratching of clawed feet running on rock, but these sounds were receding, and the activities appeared unorganized.

He walked to the beginning of the hallway and looked into the main corridor. It was deserted and the lights were dimmer. He crept down the passage until he passed his imprisonment room and reached the corner around which the blue bird had vanished. He found himself in a chamber lighted by overhead lamps shaped like upended pyramids. He sneered at the odd, perch-like furniture. Neither a bird nor a single homely feather was in sight. This was much to his liking.

He wandered to a wall chest and prowled inside for clothing. All he found was ugly pots and pans and bowls. He scattered these around the room, slammed the lid shut, and sat down on the box.

He was going to burn the first gray or white Pharsey that came in, and stick its head on a watch chain. Those birds were almost too much for even *him* to stomach.

Most Pharseys made enemies and coin, usually by dishonest means. This included everything from petty stealing to planetary wide plundering. They also sold the sad little blue, lesser intelligent (According to the white Pharseys.) birds as slaves to anyone, or thing, that had enough conklin.

There was evidence, though not enough for an arrest, until now, that Calooh was the leader of the crooked Pharseys.

This was why Beal hadn't understood how their planet was allowed into the Galactic Gathering, even on a probationary basis.

It was also why he balked so hard when the impossible occurred and Calooh was made his Second. He garnered no success with his protests, as usual. Higher Officers at Galaxy Control mysteriously insisted.

He could only go along, if he wished to keep his job. And he wasn't about to allow Calooh to obtain *that*! If that pariah bird were to run the Territorial Police for much longer—Oh! Death of Law and Order!

Beal headed for a door to his left. It opened into a great circular chamber. Different colored drapes hung from the ceiling, dividing the room into sections.

He ripped a large black drape down and wrapped it around himself, toga style, using a strip from a red drape to fasten it at the waist. Feeling less exposed, he hunted through the drapes until he discovered another door. This led to what appeared to be a bathing area.

There were several Earth Cats lounging on pillows by the huge tanks of water. The ill fated felines were grooming themselves or licking at bowls of smelly food.

Beal grunted.

Pharseys raised thousands of cats.

On Earth, it was common practice for cats to eat birds, when they could pounce on one. With Pharseys like Calooh, the cats were used as seasoning on everything the birds ate and drank.

It was disgusting to think about.

He circled around the bathing tanks, toward another door. One cat, a gray, tiger-stripe type, rubbed against his legs and purred. He became sick with pity for it and pushed it away. He stepped through the door. The cat padded along beside him. He shoved it away several times. It kept returning. He finally reached down and scratched it behind the ears. "Stick with me," he said. If he could just recall what Earth people named them. "*Fido*! And you won't be bird food!"

The cat ran ahead of him.

"Hold off doing that unless you plan to warn me about the enemy," Beal said.

The cat dropped back and looked up at him.

Beal shrugged. "That's the way it's got to be, Fido," he said. He peeked around the edge of an open door and smiled. Just outside the building, on a short, cement runway, there was an air car, bathed in glorious sunlight. This tickled him pink, until he discovered the vile hole blasted through the self-recharging power pack. He kicked the side of the car with the ball of his foot.

The cat hissed and spat on the vehicle.

"You and I are going to get along just fine, Fido," Beal said. "Let's see if we can find, maybe, another of these. One that functions." He shook his pistol at the sky. "If I could only get my hands on that worm slurping bird!" He and the cat slogged through the long grass beside the runway. He heard water lapping against rocks. "Calooh *would* strand me on his *island*!" he complained. "When I get back to Central, I'm gonna strangle that Secretary of mine and hurl his wretched body into a black hole! Cut out of work early and leave *me* to be whackowed!"

The cat romped into the grass until Beal couldn't see him. "Don't wander too far, Fido," he said, "or I'll have to abandon you when I escape this hell hole." The cat was back before he took another step. "I always did say Earth Cats were smart," he told it. "How

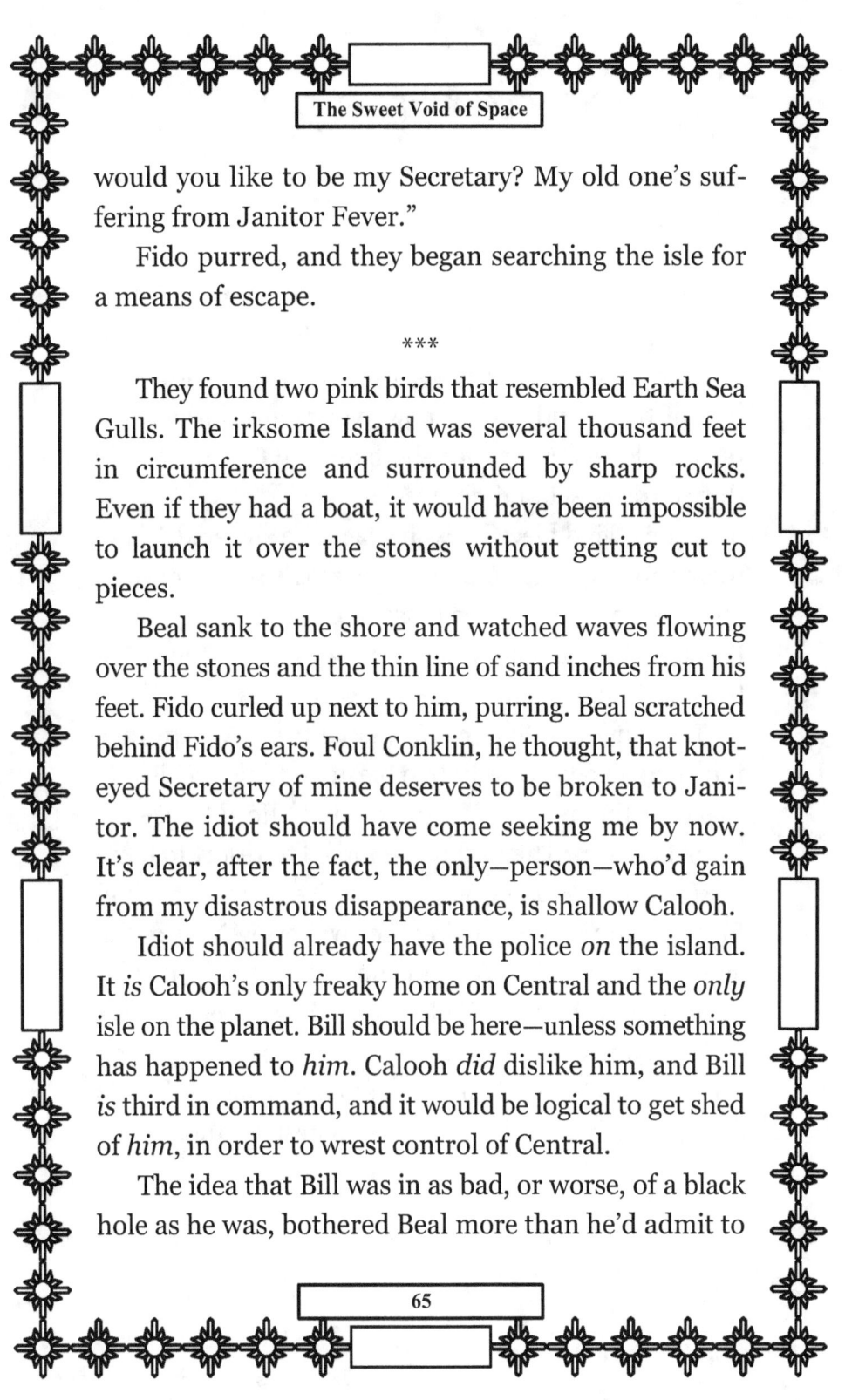

would you like to be my Secretary? My old one's suffering from Janitor Fever."

Fido purred, and they began searching the isle for a means of escape.

***

They found two pink birds that resembled Earth Sea Gulls. The irksome Island was several thousand feet in circumference and surrounded by sharp rocks. Even if they had a boat, it would have been impossible to launch it over the stones without getting cut to pieces.

Beal sank to the shore and watched waves flowing over the stones and the thin line of sand inches from his feet. Fido curled up next to him, purring. Beal scratched behind Fido's ears. Foul Conklin, he thought, that knot-eyed Secretary of mine deserves to be broken to Janitor. The idiot should have come seeking me by now. It's clear, after the fact, the only—person—who'd gain from my disastrous disappearance, is shallow Calooh.

Idiot should already have the police *on* the island. It *is* Calooh's only freaky home on Central and the *only* isle on the planet. Bill should be here—unless something has happened to *him*. Calooh *did* dislike him, and Bill *is* third in command, and it would be logical to get shed of *him*, in order to wrest control of Central.

The idea that Bill was in as bad, or worse, of a black hole as he was, bothered Beal more than he'd admit to anyone. He wasn't quite as tough or as mean as he acted. Although he hated for anyone to say as much. And he did like Bill. Bill had told him so quite often.

The boy seemed worthless, at first sight. But, if he ever left Central, the place would fold up. He and Bill were some unnatural type of team. Strange how neither of them understood how everything worked correctly only when they were both around Central. It was the weirdest fact of their lives.

A chill wind blew across his face. He shivered. There was probably a storm brewing over the water, beyond the horizon. Where *have* those birds gone, he thought? Probably to Calooh, wherever *he* is. And they'll be back, in force.

He had just one gun. Not much fire power, if they returned armed with mobile blasters. Since the island was near the mainland, they couldn't afford to use the mega beamers. They would be forced to resort to hand held units, just as he was. He noticed the pistol had fully recharged itself, using the sweltering light of the sun. Trust Calooh to arm his hordes with illegal, self--charging ordinance. Well, at least he was better prepared against the Pharseys, now. He tapped Fido on the head and started back to Calooh's palace, with his confiscated blaster turned to its highest setting.

Chapter 11
Item by Item

At dusk, Timmorey headed them back toward his cabin, at a fast pace, the long way, circling the west side of the small lake. He was still following the trail of the Pharseys.

Bill, blissfully unaware of this, was relieved they were returning to the man's cabin. He checked over his shoulder every few steps. "Is it safer out here, at night?" he asked.

"No," Timmorey assured him. "Especially if those Pharseys haven't gone off planet, or are waiting in ambush, along our trail, or at my cabin."

Bill felt the lump reforming in his throat. "Can we move faster?" he said. "And use a path they won't."

Timmorey increased their speed. "Do you know what an Item is, exactly?" he asked.

Bill shook his head. He couldn't understand how this Timmorey could move through the trees and not collide with any. He was following as close as possible without hugging the man and still had rebounded off six trees. If he did get knocked down, he didn't think he could pick himself up again, because he was so fatigued. How far away *was* that cabin, anyway?

The pace didn't bother Timmorey. "Have you ever *seen* an Item?" he asked.

Bill was winded. He shook his head.

Timmorey caught the motion. "They're a kind of living rock," he said. "They feed, in a way, on a certain type of energy found on only a few planets. They are the Guardians of the Universe Fabric. They travel the Universe emitting a solid, yet non-solid ray.

"Whenever a part of the Universe Fabric has a strain in it—and don't ask me what is straining it, because no one even pretends to know—an Item settles onto the nearest planet which is blessed with this unique energy, becomes invigorated until it glows deep purple-black, and launches into space, at speeds almost impossible to calculate. When it reaches the strain, it repairs it, even if it must sacrifice itself in the process."

They broke into a moonlit clearing. Bill sank to the grass and moss and began gasping like a locomotive.

Timmorey gave the area a thorough inspection, and returned. "Do you see those four huge circular impressions in the grass and moss around us?" he asked. "Each is a hundred feet across. The grass is matted flat in a counterclockwise swirl."

"Yeah," Bill gasped. "So?"

"This is where their saucers were," Timmorey said, as he gazed at the sky. Four purplish clouds dissipated and a quartet of pale, silver lights faded into the star field at an incredible speed. "Well," he said, "they're headed back, now, to wherever Calooh is. We'd best get to my cabin and be positive one of the white Command Birds didn't fly over there and find *my* Item."

"Wait!" Bill said. "Why's Calooh want them?"

"There is a method of controlling the Items so they will do your bidding," Timmorey said. "They can synthesize any element that exists. Losing one wouldn't be so bad, but Calooh has *five*. Major Ones. He needs one more, of any size, to be able to do what he plans, and *I* have it. There is a giant Strain in the Fabric, now, and Calooh is unwittingly, or on purpose, jeopardizing the Universe by keeping the stolen Items under wraps."

Bill found all of this hard to comprehend, let alone believe. "Can't your Item repair the—Strain?" he asked.

"No, it's a Minor One. This Strain is the greatest we've ever known. All the Items Calooh has, may not be enough," Timmorey said. He indicated the stars with a wave of his hand. "There are other Items out there, but they can't possibly reach the Strain before it blows. If we can get to Calooh, the six we'll have will be sufficient to control the Strain, until the other Items arrive to aid them in repairing it." He stood up. "Come on, we've wasted enough time."

Alderbrian Press

Bill wearily followed.

***

They entered the cabin at seven o'clock.

Timmorey thought nothing was amiss until he saw the molted blue feather half under the cot. Proof of, otherwise, artful trespass.

Bill didn't even think of being suspicious. He simply dropped into a chair and stretched out.

Timmorey removed his ammo belt and took the rifle and the small box of shells from Bill. He folded the bear rug double and opened the trap door. He got his big shell box off the dining table and clumped down the wooden stairs. After he stowed the gear on a shelf, he checked far back in the root cellar.

Bill heard things being moved under the floor.

"They didn't find it," Timmorey said, with glee, as he emerged. "That'll torque old Calooh off, for sure!" He closed the trapdoor and put the rug into its proper place. He locked the cabin door, dropped the key into his pocket, then shoved the hickory beam into its brackets. "It's time to take the offensive," He said. He unlocked and opened the teleporter. As far as he could tell, from its gleaming instruments, no one had been through. He switched off the Automatic Return and beckoned.

"Can't we rest more?" Bill complained. "I won't be worth slime to you, all tired out!"

"Hop in here!" Timmorey ordered. He spoke with a

sound of authority unlike anything Bill had ever heard or ever wanted to hear again. "You can nap *later*!"

Bill complied with haste.

Timmorey pulled the door shut and locked it with the Thumb Print Scanner built into the knob. He rubbed his beard. "Where were you before you landed here?" he asked.

"A place called the Temple of Thought, on Central," Bill said. He eyed the crowded panel and the button Timmorey was about to punch. "Why?" he asked, nervously.

Timmorey tapped the button. "Did it look like this?" he said.

Their backs were against the rear wall of the main room of the temple, just beyond the alcove with the beaded curtain.

Hundreds of people were milling about.

The Dalph prodded his way to them, stored his Teleporter Alert Sensor in his slacks pocket and smiled at Bill. "Wondered where *you'd* gotten to," he said. He faced Timmorey, in a challenging manner. "Who's your friend?" he asked Bill.

"Timmorey," Timmorey said. "Would you happen to know where Calooh is, right now?"

"By the Sacred Roots of the Vision Weeds! Timmorey!" the Dalph said. "I never thought *I'd* see *you* here!" He turned angry. "There's nobody aware of where that worm slurper is! But he's ordering every bopper on the planet to shoot at Bill." He poked a finger into Bill's ribs. "I was sure you wouldn't come back from wherever you disappeared! Surprise! That bopper you bonked is after your blood, as a souvenir!"

Timmorey glanced about the temple. "Do you have a rear exit?" he said.

"Just a Secret Emergency Ground Car Tunnel," the Dalph said, smugly. "It'll take you straight to the main lines. I'll open the hatch for you. It's in the rear wall. One of the regular cars'll come. I got gypped by the conklin grabber who built it. He stole the private car I'd ordered. Never could find that fiend." He led the way through the crowd. "Seems like that bird has gone loogy with power. Hope you don't get caught. Somebody's gotta kick him outta his high, shitty perch!" He slipped a small, metal transmitter out of his slacks pocket and pressed its button. A section of the wall popped back, then slid aside. A ground car appeared in front of them. Timmorey leaped into it.

Bill hesitated. "Has anything been heard about Beal?" he asked hopefully.

The Dalph shook his head. "The boppers figure he's been killed," he said. He turned away unhappily, with what looked, to Bill, like tears in his eyes. "Luck," he bade them. He pressed his control button and the secret entrance sealed with a snap, leaving no evidence of its existence.

Bill sat down thoughtfully.

Timmorey punched buttons on the lighted dash, then settled into the seat. "You worried about Beal?" he said.

"Yeah," Bill mumbled.

"I wouldn't be, Beal can take care of himself, no matter where he is."

Bill was surprised. "You *know* Beal?" he said.

"Quite well."

"He sure didn't act like it when Calooh was on him about you. Or even before."

Timmorey laughed. "Do you tell Beal about all your friends and everything you're involved with?" he said.

"No," Bill said. "But, the least he could do is warn me every time Calooh is coming around, so I can duck that walking stink. My life would be grossly easier, *if* Beal would deign to let me in on a few things." He rubbed the top of his head. "When did you meet him?"

"Before I took over the Earth Watch," Timmorey said. "I traveled a lot around the planetary systems with him. He was with me once when I saw one of the Items repairing a Strain. It was the only time he ever admitted he was afraid, afraid of what was behind the Strain.

"We promised each other we'd never allow any one person, or group, to control more than two of the Items, if we could manage it. Old Calooh must have pulled a slick one on him. I hope—"

"What's wrong?" Bill asked, peering all around them, through the domed top of the car.

"Where would Calooh take Beal to keep him out of his way?"

It was difficult, but Bill lost himself in thought. He knew the creepy bird had a weird palace somewhere. This is where Calooh claimed to perform all the work he failed to do for Central. Work which Bill was required to complete. He wasn't sure of the location of the palace. He closed his eyes and concentrated on the scraps of files he'd seen about Calooh. Ahh! The palace was called the Purple Perch, and it was on an island. Which one? There was only one: The Isle of Bliss, Calooh called it. All Pharsey property had silly names. He cogitated harder and culled up a mental image of the outside of the palace. That's where Calooh'd stick Beal: the Isle of Bliss. He sat up straight.

Timmorey looked bemused.

"What's wrong?" Bill asked.

"We've been captured."

Bill hadn't noticed the car had stopped. They were surrounded by policemen, including the one to whom Bill had given the lump. "What do we do?" he asked shakily.

"Give up," Timmorey said. "Until we catch an opportunity to escape." He popped the clear top open and stood up, holding his hands above his head. "Who's in charge here?" he demanded.

The policeman Bill had tangled with stepped forward. "I am," he snarled, glaring at Bill. "Why?"

"We surrender," Timmorey said.

"Whaddya mean, *we*?" the bopper snapped.

Timmorey raised his eyebrows. Calooh apparently hadn't gotten around to monitoring the teleporters yet. He scratched his beard. "I'm his lawyer," he said brusquely.

"What's he need *you* for?" the crooked bopper said. "He's already been tried *and* convicted *and* sentenced!"

Timmorey gambled. If the trial had been as Bill had described, it might work. "There hasn't *been* any trial," he snapped back. "I haven't *seen* a holo of it. This man is *free* until one is arranged!"

The shifty policeman choked on the words. "You checked, huh?" he said. "Smart guy. We still got a *pure* complaint against him." He motioned for Bill to step from the car.

Timmorey shook his head at Bill. "I haven't *seen* a copy of *any* complaint against *my* client," he said. "You can't arrest him without a warrant. Nor can you shoot him on sight, even if ordered to, if it would endanger an innocent life, *mine*." He turned nasty. "Cede our right of way and don't bother us again unless you have a warrant in your hand!" he commanded. Then he sat down with his arms folded, staring into the eyes of the

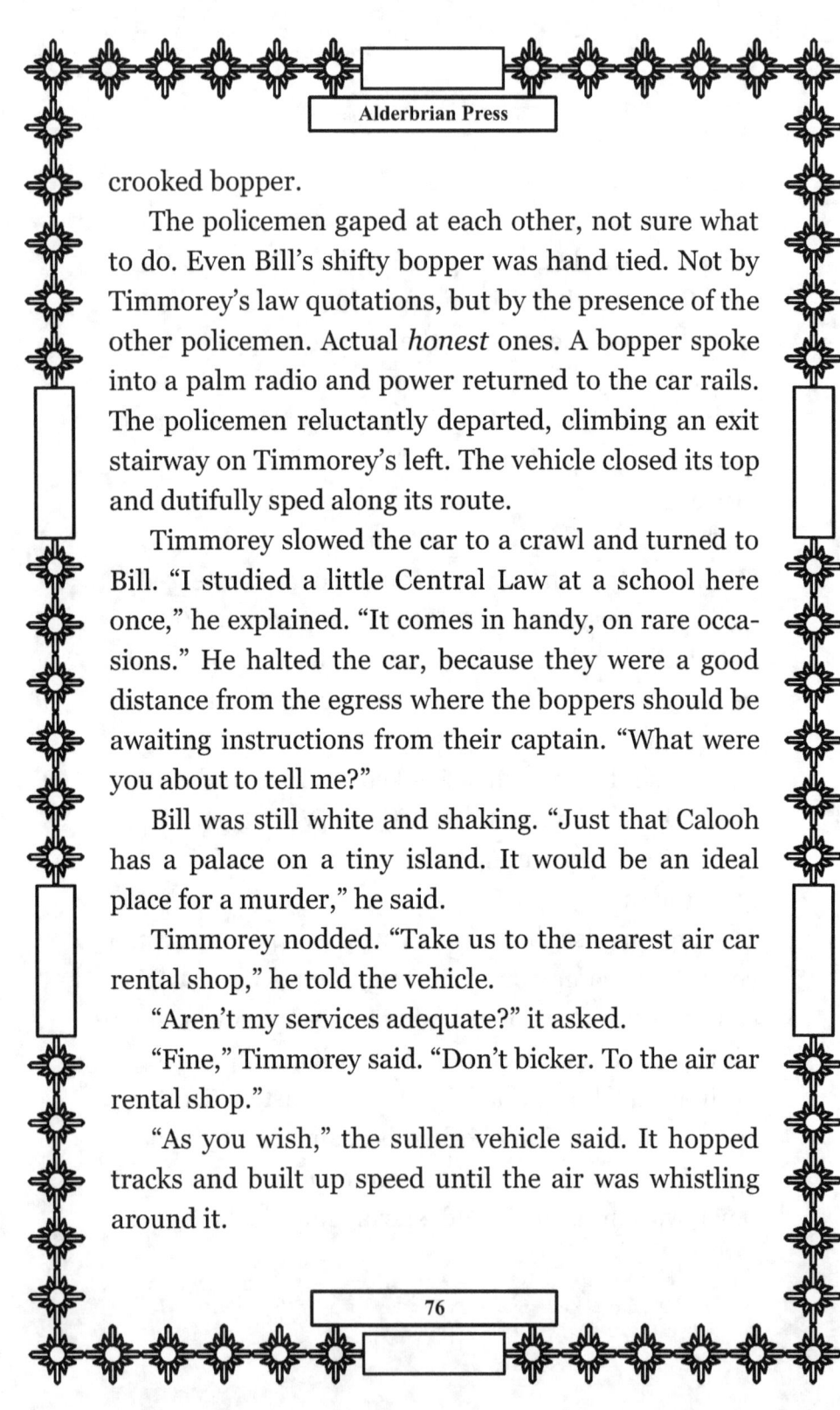

crooked bopper.

The policemen gaped at each other, not sure what to do. Even Bill's shifty bopper was hand tied. Not by Timmorey's law quotations, but by the presence of the other policemen. Actual *honest* ones. A bopper spoke into a palm radio and power returned to the car rails. The policemen reluctantly departed, climbing an exit stairway on Timmorey's left. The vehicle closed its top and dutifully sped along its route.

Timmorey slowed the car to a crawl and turned to Bill. "I studied a little Central Law at a school here once," he explained. "It comes in handy, on rare occasions." He halted the car, because they were a good distance from the egress where the boppers should be awaiting instructions from their captain. "What were you about to tell me?"

Bill was still white and shaking. "Just that Calooh has a palace on a tiny island. It would be an ideal place for a murder," he said.

Timmorey nodded. "Take us to the nearest air car rental shop," he told the vehicle.

"Aren't my services adequate?" it asked.

"Fine," Timmorey said. "Don't bicker. To the air car rental shop."

"As you wish," the sullen vehicle said. It hopped tracks and built up speed until the air was whistling around it.

***

The car entered sunlight and slowly decelerated to a stop. "Pay me," it said.

Timmorey looked at Bill. "You have any conklin?" he asked.

"The Dalph took that when he took my clothes."

"Pay me!" the car insisted. It sounded angry.

Timmorey reached into his jeans pocket and pulled out a jackknife. "See how much you can sell this for," he said, handing it to Bill.

"Regulation 5080 states—"

"Change is being obtained," Timmorey told the vehicle. "Don't blow your emotion crystals."

The car fell silent.

Timmorey watched Bill talking and gesturing to the clerk in the air car rental shop. They shook hands and the exchange was made. Bill returned and handed over a sack of coins. Timmorey fed six into the dash slot.

"Thank you, sir," the sullen car said.

Timmorey got out and counted the remaining money. "*Ten bucks!*" he said. "How'd you manage *that*? It cost me only ninety-eight cents, tax included!"

"I told him it was an antique from Earth," Bill said, trying to act embarrassed. "He seemed awfully gullible. I couldn't help taking advantage of him. He asked about my clothes. I said we'd just got back from studying customs and dress on Earth and hadn't had time to change to Central togs yet. Research for a movie. Did I do any harm?"

"The police haven't had time to get a warrant for you or me and so haven't broadcast our descriptions over public address modes. Probably won't, if sneaky Calooh wants us on the quiet," Timmorey said. "No harm, so far."

They stepped into the air car rental shop.

The clerk nodded acknowledgment to Bill and smiled. "What can I do for you?" he said.

Timmorey thumbed through a receipt book. "How much to rent one of your cars for the day?" he asked.

"For what's *left* of today—eight conklin," the clerk said. "Unless you intend to use it tonight." He pulled a laser pen from his shirt pocket.

"What time do we have to bring it back today?" Bill asked.

The clerk scratched his head with the pen. "Since I halfway know you," he said to Bill, "I'd guess, no later than seven o'clock." He filled out a receipt.

Timmorey agreed with a nod and a smile.

Bill signed the paper.

Timmorey forked over the conklin, leaving them with about a dime. He stuck their copy of the receipt into his shirt pocket and he and Bill went out onto the takeoff-landing-parking field.

"Which one is ours, Bill?"

"Number ten."

It was battered, but it would fly. For a while, they hoped.

Bill took the controls. "Little Eddy?" he asked.

"Little Eddy," Timmorey confirmed.

Chapter 12
Two's Enough

Beal triggered his blaster, melted a hole in a wall near a slave bird, and retreated into the bathing area. Fido ran ahead of him, mewing in terror. He grabbed the cat up and charged into the round room of hanging drapes. He beamed one, setting them all ablaze. This activated the recessed sprinkler system, and a fire alarm that sounded like a monstrous bird shrieking. He raced down the main corridor, scaring several blue Pharseys into flight.

He'd have to find a hiding place with immediate, easy detection of the enemy and a fast escape route. He heard squeaky voices coming from the bisecting hall ahead and dodged through a doorway. He found himself in an empty grain bin. A ramp led to a higher level. He closed the door, set his blaster to its highest level, and sealed the portal by melting it around the frame. Then he followed the ramp up to an open courtyard. This was covered by grass and cluttered with ugly statues of Pharseys in ridiculous poses. Despite the emergency situation, he stopped, let Fido go, and belly laughed.

Fido purred.

Mercifully, the fire alarm ceased, but bird guards skittered around outside the door of the grain bin.

Beal cut across the courtyard, twisting his way between the statues, until he reached an archway. The room before him had a vaulted ceiling and the floor was at least two hundred feet square. There were other archways in the walls. The one he chose led to a room where six large, white eggs lay under the clear plastic domes of metal incubators. He passed these to a door. Closing this behind him, he found himself in an antechamber with a stone chair and a stairway.

He climbed for three flights, pulled on a ring latch and shoved a door open, cautiously entering the semicircular watch room.

Fido romped in.

Beal closed and bolted the door.

Fido mewed pitifully. He was perched on a flat stone ledge. An oval, glassless window showcased the multivaulted room.

Beal went to comfort Fido.

An assortment of gray and blue birds arrived below. Their gray Commander Pharsey formed them into groups, directing each team through separate archways.

Two Pharseys came Beal's way. It wouldn't take them long to beam through his seal on the grain bin. He grabbed Fido up, unbolted the door of the watch room, and stepped over so he would be behind it when it was opened.

***

The gray birds tumbled through the door recklessly. Beal swung it shut with his foot and aimed his blaster at the cowering Pharseys. He noticed the collars around their thin necks and softened. He motioned for them to drop their weapons, then to turn around. He let Fido loose and quickly clipped both birds at the bases of their necks, with the side of his hand, knocking them unconscious. They were a sorry sight, sprawled on the floor. He tightened his grip on his gun, took up one of theirs, and ran down the stairway. Something metallic clattered behind.

Fido had the handle of the third blaster in his mouth, dragging it with obvious determination.

Beal smiled with appreciation. "Never mind that," he said. "Two's enough. Just make sure you stick close, but out of my way."

Fido left his gun on a step and followed his friend down a side hall.

Beal trotted until he reached a bare room with a locked door at the end. The bird's he'd seen go this way must have doubled back while he was fussing with Fido. He burned the lock out and the portal swung away, allowing sunlight to pour into the dim room. He smiled. He'd found what he'd wanted, a ramp leading to the grass outside the palace. He padded back into the hallway and listened. He heard the slight rustling behind and spun around with both blasters raised. I've made my *mistake*, he thought, with panic!

Timmorey knocked the guns from Beal's hands and pinned him against a wall until he was sure Beal recognized him.

Bill crept into the room with Fido in his arms.

"Where, in *Stoth's* name, did *you* two come from?" Beal snapped.

"You're welcome," Bill said.

Beal speared him with a disdainful look. "Took you long enough!" he said. "Your usual style!"

"Stow it!" Timmorey said. He recovered the blasters and tossed one to Beal. "There's an air car outside. You and Bill climb into it and wait. *I've* got some business to conduct."

Beal grabbed Timmorey's arm. "Hold on," he said, "*I'm* gonna kill that, *nordhonger*, Calooh!"

"That's just what *I* won't allow!" Timmorey said. "We *must* compel him to reveal where he's hidden the Items he's copped. *No matter what!*" he emphasized.

"Why?" Beal said. His voice was tinged with uncertainty.

Fido mewed nervously.

"A Major Strain," Timmorey said.

Beal nodded. "You'll need help, believe me," he said, "this place is swarming with guards, and they all have these playthings." He turned to Bill. "Get inside that car and keep it idling," he said. "Take the cat!"

Bill left without a word. He knew he'd only get in the way, otherwise.

***

Timmorey and Beal ran along the hallways until they reached the multi-vaulted room. They stood next to a wall and peered around the corner.

A number of servant Pharseys was gathered in the center of the great chamber. The gray Commander listened to their reports and issued new instructions. The searchers moved down various hallways, away from the men, leaving the Commander alone.

Timmorey noted the bird was a rare, trusted associate. It wore no obedience collar. He tackled the fowl before it could squawk twice.

A moment later, Beal was next to Timmorey, clamping the Pharsey's beak shut with his free hand.

Timmorey jerked the bird to its feet. "I want two things from you!" he whispered, fiercely. "Where is Calooh? Where has he concealed the Items?"

Beal released the bill.

The Pharsey let loose a horrifying peril shriek.

Beal knocked the bird unconscious.

Timmorey laid it on the floor. "Come on!" he said.

He ducked through another archway.

Timmorey knew Calooh was a typical Pharsey and preferred high places: somewhere the fowl could view all his territory. Timmorey had seen a tower when he and Bill had flown in. If Calooh had sighted the car landing, he probably would have left by now, via a saucer, and underwater, to gather reinforcements. If not, odds were, he would be in *that* tower, expecting *only* Beal.

Beal found a flight of steps and they took them, advancing upward six levels until they reached an anteroom. The door to the main room was being guarded by ten armed, blue servant birds. Two gray Commanders stood on either side.

Beal and Timmorey pressed themselves against the wall. There were urgent squawks below and scaly feet scratched on stone as numerous Pharseys began a cautious ascent to the tower room.

"Now what?" Beal whispered, checking the setting on his blaster.

"Surrender," Timmorey said. He dropped his gun to the steps, held his hands above his head and walked into the anteroom.

"Damn!" Beal muttered, as he did likewise.

Chapter 13

A Timid Man

Bill waited for half an hour, then decided to see what was taking Beal and Timmorey so long. He shut off the engine, climbed out of the air car, and dumped the cat on the grass.

At the top of the ramp, as they walked through the blasted metal door, the silence made Fido's purring unusually loud, and unnerving.

"Stop that!" Bill whispered.

The cat fell quiet and looked up with a hurt light in his eyes.

Bill shrugged it off and continued down the corridor.

Fido sat where it was for a moment, then followed.

Bill felt uneasy and turned around.

The cat still looked sad.

"All, right," Bill said, with exasperation, "I'm *Nordhonger* sorry."

Fido rubbed against Bill's legs, purring.

Bill shook his head in wonder and proceeded. He approached a corner.

The cat hunched his back and spat.

Bill flattened against the wall and stopped breathing.

Two blue birds passed.

Fido relaxed and resumed purring.

Bill saluted the cat and led him down the new hall, away from the Pharseys.

***

Bill was lost. He looked down at the cat. "Find Beal," he said. It was more a hopeful suggestion than a harsh command.

Fido glanced around at the halls and shrugged his shoulders.

Bill slapped himself on the forehead. "Great!" he said. "We make a *fine* team! A feline with no tracking skills, and a frightened secretary, part-time janitor!" He sank to the floor. Fido crawled into his lap. "Why couldn't I be satisfied with the Refuse Room?" he asked Fido. "At least *it* was guaranteed!"

A blue Pharsey rounded a corner a few feet ahead.

Bill hid the cat behind himself and feigned what he feared he would soon be a portrait of: death.

The bird saw Bill. It peeped with apprehension but edged closer to the corpse. It stuck a gun barrel into Bill's ribs and jumped back.

Bill suppressed a grunt of pain and remained still. He couldn't hold his breath much longer.

The Pharsey glanced around, wondering what to

do.

Bill blinked both eyes.

The fowl fainted.

Bill was astounded, and his relief was so intense, it was embarrassing. He snatched up the blaster and fled with the cat, cutting aimlessly down halls, to put space between themselves and the bird.

Fido skidded to a stop.

Bill attempted to avoid stepping on the cat, slipped, and fell on his side. He sat up angrily. They had bungled into a dead end. He clutched the gun tighter, thought about the fainted Pharsey, and realized, as true, something Timmorey had said on Earth. These birds *are* cowards. They weren't interested in killing *or* being killed. They *would* rather *run* than *fight*. He grinned. When a timid man is faced with something more timid, he can be *very* brave. He growled at Fido, got up and strutted down the hall, recklessly rounding the corner.

Six blue Pharseys advanced.

Bill stood his ground and sneered.

The birds were obviously shaken by this odd behavior. They stopped several feet away, with their guns ready.

"Which of you is in charge?" Bill demanded. The tone of his voice amazed and satisfied him.

"I am," the nearest bird said, meekly. "You are our

prisoner."

Bill burned a shallow trench across the floor, from wall to wall, in front of the Pharseys. "Correction," he said. "*You* are *my* prisoners!" He melted a hole at the feet of the spokes bird. "Throw down your weapons, or I'll beam the lot of you into ashes and pour oil over them!" The latter, he recalled, was a feared sacrilege to them.

The lead bird peeped and dropped his pistol. The others followed suit.

Bill sighed with relief.

The Pharseys shuffled around nervously. The spokes bird had fear in his large blue eyes. "What do you wish us to do?" he asked, timidly.

Bill noticed the odd wire collars encircling each Pharsey's neck. He recalled what Timmorey had said about them and shuddered. What could *he* do? He concentrated for a few moments, then addressed the lead bird. "Do you have any tools around here?"

The Pharsey nodded. "Not far. Why?" he said.

"Can I trust you to fetch them, *and* return, *without* warning any others about *me*?" Bill asked. He squinted to appear cruel. "If you don't, I'll kill this bunch, then come after you!"

"I—I'll come back! I promise!" the bird said. He spoke to his companions in their twittering language, then raced around a corner.

Bill was taking a great risk. But he was pretty sure the fowl cared for his pals and would be back with the tools.

Fido was crouched and showing his fangs to the Pharseys.

The hostages began speaking among themselves and glancing at Bill.

Bill wondered if they were planning to attack en masse, hoping one or two would survive to alert Calooh.

One stepped near. "If Regley fails to return, for any reason, with what you desire, will you kill us?" he asked, obviously frightened.

Bill shook his head. "No," he said, "but, only *if* you *all* swear a *blood* oath not to hinder me, *and* not to warn Calooh that *I* am here!"

The bird rejoined the group. They held a discussion and reached an accord.

Regley reappeared, carrying a metal box. He released the ring on the top, setting the chest down.

Bill motioned the fowl back, then knelt, opened the box, and dumped its contents on the floor. The tools were strange, fashioned for tiny wing hands. The only thing he could find to serve his purpose, was a razor-sharp, needle-thin saw. He checked the power level indicator on the handle. It was fully charged. He stood up with the saw and the gun and waved Regley over to him. He grabbed the bird around the chest with his gun arm, keeping the blaster aimed at the Pharsey's companions, and raised the saw toward the fowl's throat.

"*No!*" Regley begged. "You *promised!*"

Bill shook the Pharsey. "Hold still and I'll cut that collar off," he said.

Regley blinked. "You can't," he said, with uncertainty. "The masters told us *nothing* can remove them."

"They lied," Bill said. "There's no metal known can resist a saw like this. Now, be still. And you boys better not try anything, or I might *slip!*"

Trained in Basic or not, the Pharseys caught the meaning in the tone of Bill's voice. They froze.

The instant Bill slipped the blade into place, the collar began to tighten. The saw hummed, the evil collar snapped, fell to the stone floor, and rolled into a tight ball.

Regley raised his trembling wings to his neck. His astonishment was heartwarming. His friends crowded around him with excitement.

Bill handed the saw to one of them and said, "Tell him he has to operate the saw without hesitation."

Regley nodded and translated the instructions.

Fido relaxed.

Bill picked him up.

Regley blinked with curiosity but said nothing.

Bill motioned and they moved a distance up the hall.

"Now that you are free," Bill said, "you owe nothing to Calooh. Will you lead me to him, in a way that will keep me from being discovered."

"Gladly!" Regley said. "Gratefully!"

They traveled a series of hallways until they came to a small, oven-shaped door. Bill opened it, pulling its tiny knob toward him.

Regley entered, sending his long neck snaking ahead.

Bill directed Fido in, bent almost double, and followed, closing the door and plunging them into darkness.

The tunnel took a gentle upward slope.

***

The smooth floor gave way to small steps. The only hint, to Bill, that his guide was still before him, was the sound of claws on stone. The cat was purring, and this reassured him, somewhat.

***

They entered a stuffy chamber. A thin glow outlined another oven-shaped door.

"Calooh is through here," Regley said, as if he had a foul taste in his beak. "I will now help others of my clan free themselves from their murderous, banned collars!" He vanished down the long tunnel; the scratching of his claws swiftly echoing to silence.

Bill could see the cat's eyes glinting. "You ready,

chum?" he said.

Fido purred.

Bill grasped the tiny knob and swung the door sound-
lessly open inward, allowing yellow light to stream in.

Chapter 14

Three Dead Houndas

Just below Bill's hidey hole, Calooh sat on a high, perch-like chair. Five gray Pharseys were stationed beneath his dangling claws.

A purple wooden beam projected from the far wall of the tower room. Four chains were screwed into the near end of this beam. Timmorey and Beal hung from the manacles connected to those chains.

Timmorey saw Bill's face and smiled.

Calooh glared. "What do *you* have to *smile* about?" he said, with hatred. "You are going to *die*, very soon! *Slowly* and *painfully*!" He hissed.

The center guard spun around on one foot, keeping his eyes toward the floor.

Calooh whispered to the cowering fowl.

The Pharsey nodded in an exaggerated way, marched over, and rapped its beak once against each of the iron doors. They opened outward and the frightened bird exited the room with haste.

"You see," Calooh gloated, "we make ready for you

now!"

Beal caught sight of Bill. His eyes bulged and he turned very red. He thought: Crud! Why hasn't that idiot jumped Calooh? There are *only* four guards left in the room, and they won't fire as long as he's near Calooh! What *is* he waiting for?

Calooh snaked his head with glee. "I see *you* realize your *grave* situation, Beal," he said. "Enjoy it!" He chortled and flew from his perch, alighting before the doors. He tapped on each one with his beak. The doors slowly opened for his exit, but he paused. "Watch them, most carefully," he sternly instructed the guards. "If they move more than six inches, any one way, burn their feet off! I will be at Operations Central, *if* you require me." He stalked out and the doors clanged shut.

The nervous Pharseys drew closer to each other, holding their weapons at wing's reach.

Timmorey and Beal were just inches from the floor.

Bill set the dial on his blaster. It would singe the hair on their wrists, but it would free them, and he might not have to kill the birds. He took a deep breath and carefully aimed. Energy seared from the blaster, melting the thick chains in half, and scorching an impression in the wall below the beam.

Startled speechless, the Pharseys whirled toward Bill.

Beal and Timmorey hit the floor, and a moment later, the birds lay unconscious.

Bill leaned against a wall in his smoking hidey hole. He was sweating and shaking and holding Fido behind him. One of those ugly worm slurpers had nearly *fried* them!

Timmorey noticed an electronic key lying beside one of the Pharseys and used it to unlock the manacles.

Beal scooped up two blasters, tossed one to Timmorey, then stormed over and glared up. "*That* was a *stupid* thing to do!" he said. "I thought, sure, you'd flipped *loogy*!"

"Wha—whad'ya expect me to do, dance them unarmed?" Bill said, lamely.

Beal snorted and held up his arms.

Fido glanced at Bill, then jumped to Beal.

Timmorey had an ear pressed against one of the iron doors.

"What about *me*?" Bill said.

"That's *your* problem, brain man!" Beal said.

Timmorey slipped over to stand beneath Bill's tunnel. "Can you find your way out of there, the way you came in?" he asked.

Bill shrugged, feeling uneasy. "Yeah," he said, "but —"

"Never mind," Timmorey said. "When you get out, make your way to this room and yell, ugly, as loud as you can. Don't run unless you're sure *all* the guards are after you! We'll relieve the pressure from behind."

"You're *crazy*!" Bill said. "I'm not a *hero*! I *won't* be a *gorgy* sitting Hounda!"

"Get going!" Timmorey said. "And *double time it*!"

"What?"

Timmorey growled.

"All right," Bill said resentfully. He hesitated, then stumbled down the steps and waddled along the smooth tunnel. It seemed to require forever to reach the end. He cracked open the oven shaped door and peeked out. He sighed with relief and exited the tunnel, closing it up.

"Now, where?" he mumbled.

He ran to his left, to the end of the corridor, and checked the intersecting hallway. It was mercifully empty, but a chill shot through him.

The palace was as silent as a tomb.

His tomb.

He turned right, down that corridor, to the next opening. There were a lot of hallways, connecting with a lot of other hallways.

He clenched his fists and groaned.

Lost!

Lost!

Lost!

He stood in the center of the intersection, spat into the palm of one hand, and brought the other fist down onto it. He curled his upper lip in disgust, wiped the spit-

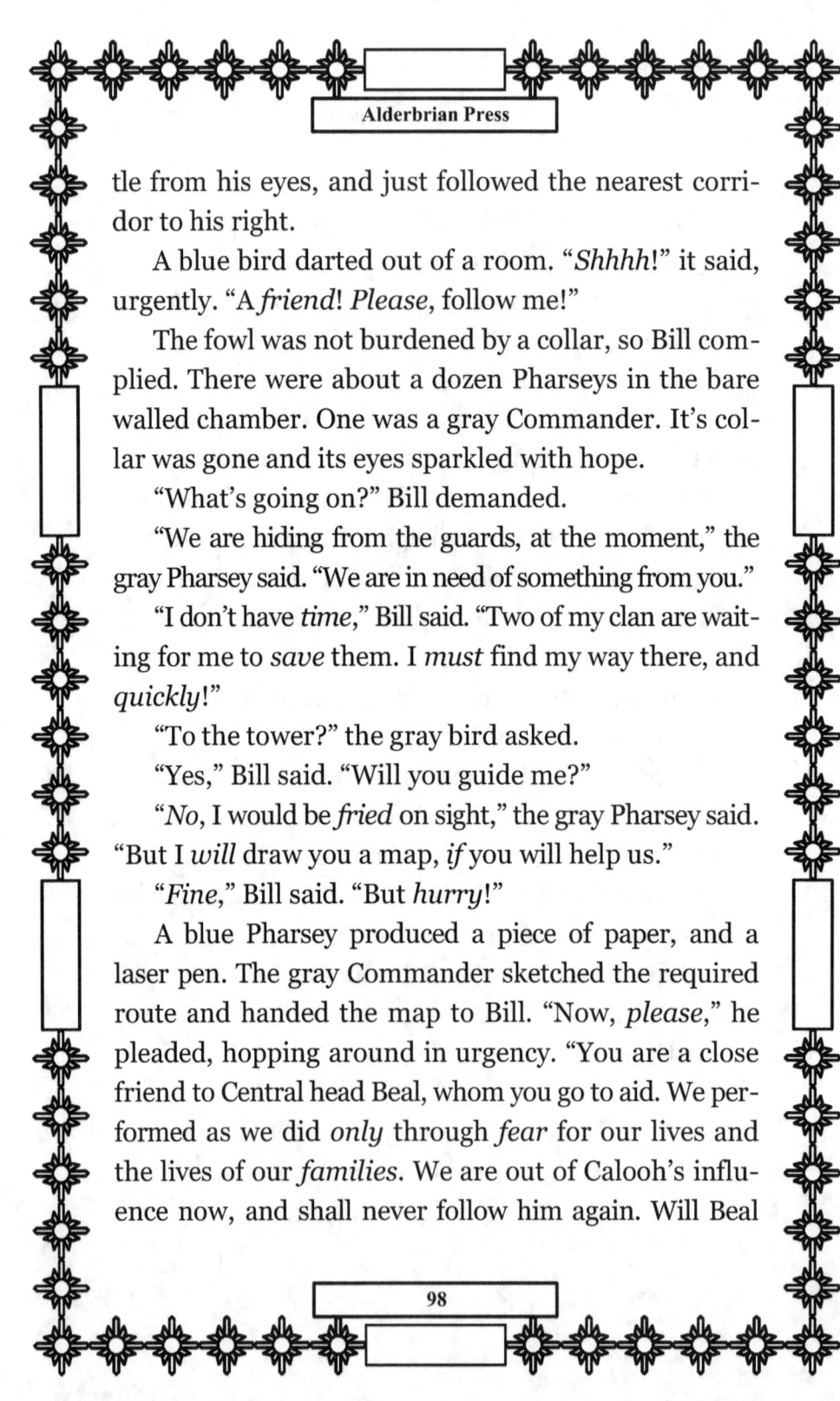

tle from his eyes, and just followed the nearest corridor to his right.

A blue bird darted out of a room. "*Shhhh!*" it said, urgently. "A *friend! Please*, follow me!"

The fowl was not burdened by a collar, so Bill complied. There were about a dozen Pharseys in the bare walled chamber. One was a gray Commander. It's collar was gone and its eyes sparkled with hope.

"What's going on?" Bill demanded.

"We are hiding from the guards, at the moment," the gray Pharsey said. "We are in need of something from you."

"I don't have *time*," Bill said. "Two of my clan are waiting for me to *save* them. I *must* find my way there, and *quickly!*"

"To the tower?" the gray bird asked.

"Yes," Bill said. "Will you guide me?"

"*No*, I would be *fried* on sight," the gray Pharsey said. "But I *will* draw you a map, *if* you will help us."

"*Fine*," Bill said. "But *hurry!*"

A blue Pharsey produced a piece of paper, and a laser pen. The gray Commander sketched the required route and handed the map to Bill. "Now, *please*," he pleaded, hopping around in urgency. "You are a close friend to Central head Beal, whom you go to aid. We performed as we did *only* through *fear* for our lives and the lives of our *families*. We are out of Calooh's influence now, and shall never follow him again. Will Beal grant us amnesty?"

"*Guaranteed!*" Bill said. He exited the room, ran down some halls and turned left into another. He veered right and stood in the doorway of a chamber. He checked the map, crossed through the room and went into the corridor beyond. He followed this until he came to the correct access.

He stared up at the six flights of steep stairs and groaned. By the time he reached the tower sentries, he'd be too weary to flee far, before passing out.

"If I don't get killed," he promised himself, "I'm going to retire from Central and manage a noodle making shop. I can't nose into any trouble doing that!"

***

Bill crept up the final flight of stairs.

There were still ten armed blue birds and two gray Officer Pharseys in front of the tower room.

And me without guts, Bill thought. What Nordhonger odds! He took a deep breath, then another, then he stepped away from the stairway wall. Easily making an appropriate face, he screamed:

"Uuuuu-gaaaa-leeee!"

The guards peeped and squawked, sounding like an out of control cheer leading squad, and began firing in different directions, missing Bill.

The iron doors burst open, knocking the Pharseys flat of their necks, sideways, in both directions. Beal and Timmorey charged along the landing and down the steps. Bill, although he was nearly exhausted, did not lag behind.

***

By the time the tower birds were in possession of their wits and half organized, the men were in the air car and soaring over Little Eddy.

Timmorey thumbed a button on the dash. "What time is it?" he asked.

The car cleared its speaker with gross sounding static. "It is now six thirty-two and one half," it said. "You sly *gilgos* will have to hurry *if* you intend to return me to my *litigious* boss man *on* time. Thank you."

Timmorey released the button.

"Turn around!" Beal shouted. "Turn this heap around! I forgot Fido!" He reached past Bill's nose and punched at the controls.

The car came about with a whine.

Timmorey slapped Beal's hands away from the buttons and wheel. "*What's* gotten into *you*?" he said. "We don't have much fly time left. That cat can *wait*." He returned the whining vehicle to its original heading.

Beal slumped back in his seat, glaring out the window on his side.

Bill glanced from one to the other of his friends and shrugged. He scratched his bald head and remembered his fake face hair. He pulled the mustache and beard off and stuck them to the clear top of the car. Then he rubbed his chin and upper lip until the last of the cheap adhesive balled up and fell on the floor. "What are we gonna do?" he asked. "Calooh'll have his guards all over Central. He may even have boppers hiding in the waste paper receptacles. We'll need something to fight with!"

"The three blasters we brought will be more than sufficient," Timmorey said. He reached behind, into the luggage compartment, and felt around. "About that cat," he said, "did it resemble this?" He handed Fido over.

Beal held the cat up and smiled. "I should have *known*," he said. "You're as *sneaky* as I am!"

Fido began purring.

Timmorey located the blasters and checked the lighted charge-level indicators and the beam settings on their dials. He glanced side wise at Bill. "You ever been a Janitor?" he asked.

Bill *and* Beal stiffened.

"Wha—what do you *mean*?" Bill stammered. Foul memories were causing him to shake.

"Just what I said," Timmorey replied. He scratched his jaw. "Is there any way into Central, other than the front doors?"

"There's a supply chute," Beal said. "But it has a robot accepting device. You wouldn't live long, after entering."

"Nothing else?" Timmorey said. "How about fire escapes, in case all those records catch fire from your temper?"

The car slowed for a landing.

Beal smiled and shook his head. "Sprinklers and foam to frustrate the biggest inferno," he said. "Besides, we can teleport out faster, even when the power fails, because they have multi-redundant backup power cells."

The vehicle circled the nearly dark field and settled down. Its tinny speaker crackled to life. "You have four seconds fly-time left and *are* due a refund," it said. "Do you wish to claim it?"

"No," Timmorey said, pushing Bill's hand from the dash coin slot.

"Thank you, sir," the car said. "Come again, often. Every day, if you can."

They stepped from the vehicle. It glided to a parking stall and sighed like a human more than ready for a long rest.

Beal and Timmorey felt guilty about the way they had fought over its steering wheel, forcing the battered old vehicle to work harder than it should have.

The attendant came out of the shop. He scrutinized Beal intensely. "Ain't you that movie—"

"Yeah," Beal said quickly, with a frown. "Keep it under your tongue and I'll pray for you tonight."

The attendant chuckled. He pointed to Beal's toga. "That tog-about ain't the most conventional style a sane man's ever seen," he said. He patted Fido on the head.

"We just finished holographing a movie about an insane mentalist who travels through time and space and dimensions and talks to upside down ghosts," Timmorey said. "And, cogitate this, he wears baggy trousers and a blue sweat shirt!"

The attendant chuckled. "Sounds like a real bagooney holo-hummer," he said. "What do you fancy skucks play in it?"

"I was an Earth Roman Emperor," Beal said. "In the holo-movie, I'm just winding up an orgy, when the mentalist appears on a table and begins preaching about the foolishness of nudity and the equality of all sentient beings. It's a cosmo-gas when a clutch of dancing girls drag him off, screaming, into their dressing room." Being an administrator, Beal was hard put for imagination.

"What were you two?" the attendant asked, goggling again at Timmorey's and Bill's blue jeans and checked shirts.

"We were a couple of Earthmen," Timmorey said hastily.

"*No*! You *actually* had to *act* like *Earthmen*!" the attendant said. "What a *riot*!" He leaned against Bill until he stopped guffawing. Then he wiped away a tear. "You guys must be *swell* actors!"

"Thanks," Timmorey mumbled, trying hard not to feel insulted. "Hey," he added. "We don't get paid until the end of the week. Could you lend us enough coin to reach the Temple of Thought, in a ground car?"

"Sure thing," the attendant said. He struggled a hand into his jumper pants pocket. "That jackknife you sold me, you must of picked it up on Earth while you were studying the natives. I hear it's a mega-weird place. Is that true?" He handed Bill the conklin.

Timmorey whistled. "You wouldn't believe what goes on there, mister," he said. "But, we're in a hurry. We gotta get, smop, to the Temple to holograph a sequel to The Mad Mentalist. I'll tell you about Earth sometime."

"Yeah," the attendant said. "Luck on the movies."

Beal held Fido out. "Take care of my Earth cat, friend," he said. "I'll be back for him later! My Word of Stoth!"

"Sure winks, brother. He'll be fine! My Word of Stoth!" the attendant said. He went into the office, chuckling and petting the cat.

Fido was purring.

Beal flagged down a ground car and they climbed in. Bill pressed the destination buttons and sat back.

"Wonder why that clerk didn't ask about our blasters," Timmorey said.

"It's legal to carry low-yield side-arms now," Beal muttered. He was obviously unhappy about that bit of legislation. "He probably thought they were props, even though they didn't fit into the story. Movie star, indeed!" He snorted.

"Are you two *sure* there aren't any other ways into Central, than the doors and that chute?" Timmorey said.

Bill felt the pink sore on his head and tried to think. A noise not unlike the grinding of gears came from around him.

Beal became concerned. Upon further inspection, he discovered the noise was issuing from beneath the seat of the car.

Wisps of smoke began curling from under Bill.

Beal yawned, reached behind Bill, tapped Timmorey on the shoulder, and indicated the smoke.

Timmorey startled. "It's *not* possible!" he said. He jostled Bill. "What *are* you doing, *man*? The whole *cab* is on *fire*! We don't need your ideas, if it means *burning* to death!"

Bill waved a hand feebly. "I—didn't!" he protested.

The smoke began billowing from under the seat. The car switched its tinny speaker on. "Short in circuitry! Short in circuitry!" it shouted. There was an interference growl while it braked to a swift stop. "Gonna have a hot time in the old chassis *tonight*," it sang, as its brain overheated. "Three *dead* Houndas! Three *dead* Houndas! If you don't flee now, you'll be Three *dead* Houndas!" The transparent top popped open. "Explosion imminent! I'm a *goner*! Save your *lazy-ass* selves! Danger! Make superswift exit! Explosion, quicko! Gree-woooulll-reee!"

Chapter 15
That Refuse Man

Calooh sat angrily in the Administrator's chair in Beal's office. A blue Pharsey, with its head bowed in terror, was kneeling in front of the desk.

"*Escaped*!" Calooh screamed. "They were in *quadtanium* chains! How could they *escape*, unless *you* aided them?"

The bird tried to speak, to explain, to defend itself.

Calooh ignored its desperate sounds. "Guards!" he shouted.

Two gray birds entered through the open door.

Calooh swept a wing at the blue Pharsey. "Take that out and sell it!" he ordered.

The guards grabbed the servant around the neck with their small wing hands and dragged it from the office.

The Pharsey did not struggle. It was still astounded by its good fortune. It had expected to die.

Calooh jabbed at the push buttons on the desk intercom until he finally found the correct one.

A bird with a shaky voice answered.

"Place the planet on Martial Law!" Calooh ordered. "Instruct the local police to shoot Bill Wayden, and anyone with him, on sight, and not to ask questions, first! Do you understand me?"

The Pharsey at Bill's desk mumbled something in their native twitter.

Calooh laughed. "Have the ruins checked," he said hopefully. "Tell me if they are dead. Keep the police searching the planet, in any case. We'll beat them, yet, and plunder this damned world! We'll hit them so hard, they won't be sure what happened! That will tell the mighty Alderbrian and the Council of Earths, who is truly *fit* to rule! Send Faldon in!"

A white bird entered and stood respectfully before the desk.

"*Slaves!*" Calooh said suddenly to his Second in Command. "They would make *excellent* slaves for the High Clans! "Would you like a lowly man for a slave? He would bend to your every whim, say what you wanted and beg for mercy when his collar drew too tight! I would enjoy having Timmorey for *my* slave! I would choke him once a day to awaken him and force him to clean up after the felines. I would make him eat their brains raw after he slew and skinned them!" He ruffled his feathers. "It's unfortunate that I must kill him. He might make an amusing pet. I could teach him tricks." He glared at the other bird. "You did not answer me, Faldon! Would you like a *man* for a *slave*?"

"Yes," Faldon hissed. "Every right-thinking Pharsey would enjoy owning one!"

They stared across the desk at each other with mutual admiration.

Calooh had fired all Operations Central personnel, except one. He couldn't reach him. He didn't even know who the man was, just that he was afraid of him and wanted him caught.

This human worked in the Refuse Room and was hiding behind two sets of doors not easily blasted through. He had been conducting raids on the Pharseys until the servants were too terrified to venture into the basement.

Most of the birds were guarding the entrances to the cellar and allowing no one up or down.

Calooh jerked his head up and cleared his thoughts. "That Refuse man *must* be captured," he snapped. "If you succeed, and we can get a collar on him, without killing him, he shall be *your* slave."

Faldon honked. "*My* slave! *My* slave!" he said excitedly. He turned to the doorway. "I'll have him before this day is *out!*" he promised as he left.

Calooh cooed. Faldon had done him proud many times. He would do so now.

***

A blue Pharsey charged into the office and began babbling.

Calooh let it garble off its terror until it started to make sense. "Be silent!" he ordered. He flew from his chair and strode to the bird. "What has happened?" he demanded.

"Faldon is gone!" it shouted, leaping from foot to foot.

"Where?" Calooh shouted. His heart was thudding with fear. "How?"

"We were going to execute your orders to Faldon when a big man jumped out of nowhere. He pointed a hand held machine at Faldon and Faldon just disappeared! The man chased me, but I soared down a hallway and around a corner before he could use his device on me! There was nothing I could do, Great One! He just aimed his horrible machine and, poof, Faldon was gone!"

"Shut up!" Calooh hissed. Fear turned his beak red. "Shut up and get out of here! Go hide, but get out!"

The Pharsey fled the office.

Calooh leaned weakly against a wall. Faldon hadn't even had time to reorganize the guards and get them started on the capture. The man must have been listening to or watching them. But how? None of the sentries have reported seeing him, yet. They all are at their stations. He could not pass them, so he must have some secret way into each room in Control. He reached a decision. He whistled three times.

An Officer bird entered and stood at attention with its head bowed.

"Madron, order additional guards from my father," Calooh said. "Tell him my life is in danger. We must have the maximum number he can spare, at the earliest opportunity!"

Madron bowed and left.

Calooh called to one of the four gray guards stationed just outside the door. "Gather a sentry from every post and search the entire complex for any hidden passages and trapdoors," he ordered. "You will be in charge of the operation. Shoot anyone of unauthorized presence."

The bird nodded and exited.

Calooh stepped out of the office. "Come with me," he said to the three gray Pharseys still guarding the door. He led them to Beal's sleeping quarters. He posted two outside and one inside, then settled on the bed and fell asleep.

***

Calooh was awakened by a very slight grating noise. He craned his neck and gaped around the room. Then he squawked with rage. His inside guard was gone! A moment later, the door opened and the outer sentries skittered in to see what was wrong.

Calooh rolled off the bed.

There was a piece of orange paper lying on the floor where the guard had stood. It bore a message scrawled in very purple ink:

To: Usurper Calooh.

You sure ain't gonna like what I got to say, <u>Nordhonger</u>! But, if you don't cleverly surrender the whereabouts of those Items you pilfered, and clear outta here in a couple hours, I'm gonna continue stealing your soldiers until you're all alone and helpless, then I'm gonna pluck your scummy hide and send you into the street, naked as a non-beaked Groop-Walli! Best do as I command! <u>Nordhonger</u>!

From: Killroy Killareen Kalakatoosee

Calooh stood still. His beak turned red through fear. The guards nearly went to pieces at his behavior. He noted this and controlled himself somewhat. "Form a security circle for me," he said to the closest Pharsey.

The bird ran from the room. It returned seconds later with several gray fowl and they surrounded their master.

"The one who kills this Refuse man, if he attacks, receives my palace on the Isle of Bliss, everything it contains, *and* freedom!" Calooh said. He was escorted to Beal's office by ultra-alert, hyper-eager sentries, without incident. They remained with him while he shouted orders over the building-wide speaker system.

A gray Pharsey burst into the office. It was shaking with terror and gasping for breath. "Madron is gone!" it squawked.

"When?" Calooh demanded.

"Moments ago!" the bird said. "We just supplicated your father for the reinforcements over the Holo-Com Phone and were returning to report his agreement. A big, hairy human leaped around a corner and hit Madron with a ray from some machine. Madron vanished! He didn't even have time to scream! When I and some of the other guards blasted at him, the man just laughed and leaped back around the corner. *But*, he wasn't there, seconds later, when we pursued! *And*, we couldn't find *any* secret doors!"

Before Calooh could react, other birds, gray and blue, began reporting Pharseys missing throughout the huge complex. The Refuse man was implementing his plan with swift competency, yet he had been seen only twice.

Calooh was certain the man had intended to be seen then. He stormed back and forth before the desk, hissing and spitting and waiting for the reinforcements from his father.

***

No new birdnappings were reported and the complex quieted. The white Pharseys began re-posting the terror-grouped sentries.

A message arrived: The extra guards were on the

planet and en route to Operations Central.

Calooh became calm. He thought: That slithering, evil man can't elude capture, forever. We'll get him *yet*! Especially with the aid of the expert Officers coming with father's reinforcements! He perched on the seat of Beal's chair.

A gray bird beak-knocked on the door jamb and trotted in.

Calooh looked up sharply. "What is it?" he said with irritation.

"The analysis on those car ruins," the fowl reported. "They weren't killed in the explosion. No evidence of bones or teeth was found. What do you wish now?"

Calooh's beak turned pink for a moment. "Double the search effort by the police outside," he ordered. "Don't let them stop until—No! Kill the other two, but capture Timmorey! There is something he has, that I desire. I need it badly. If he is slain, you, and everyone else involved in his death, will be incinerated and their ashes thrown into rancid oil!"

Chapter 16
The Hard Part

Bill and his friends raced into the Temple of Thought. Several policemen fired their blasters and melted large scars in the stone floor just a hair's breadth behind.

The main chamber was buzzing with people seeking refuge from the turmoil building in the streets.

Bill, Timmorey and Beal wound their way through the throng.

The Dalph sighted them and prodded his way over. He and Beal embraced.

"I thought you'd been killed, Edmondo," the Dalph said. "But I should have known better."

Beal silenced him with a look. "Let's get somewhere we can talk," he said. "We don't have very much time, I'd judge."

The Dalph led them to the room with the curtain of red, soundproof beads where Bill had been kept and clipped. He sat on the edge of the cot and frowned. "The whole planet's on Martial Law," he said, "and swarming with wild boppers looking to *kill* you three."

"We know, brother," Beal said. "Six of them grazed the tunnel where we entered the Temple."

"Blessed Stoth!" the Dalph said. He rubbed his hands together with relish. "I can raise, if you'll pardon the expression, holy hell with them over *that*! They were on Temple land when they fired!"

Bill couldn't help himself, he grinned at Beal. "Edmondo, huh?" he said. "You *must* be kidding!"

"That's my first name," Beal said. "The last one who laughed at it, is now a Janitor."

Bill winced. "I take it you two know each other," he said. "Any thing you'd like to tell me?"

"We're acquainted," Beal said. "The Dalph is my brother. I've stood his face for thirty years. That's why I'm the way I am."

Bill marveled at the spooky combination. One brother was the Chief Law Enforcement Officer of the planet, the other ran a legal sanctuary for law breakers! He felt dizzy.

"Never mind history," Timmorey said. "I still want into Central before late tonight. I'm going to try to enter through the sewer outlet of the Refuse Room. I'll need a few things first." He scratched his beard thoughtfully.

Beal closed his mouth with a shaky hand. "You can't go in *there*!" he protested. "The rubbish that comes out of *that* pipe will burn you to a *crisp*?"

"I know," Timmorey said. "Can you obtain me some fire wear? I want an Earth Boomerang, too. You know what it is? And a small, but very strong flashlight."

The Dalph nodded. "I can manage," he said, as he pushed through the beads.

"I take it, you're entering *alone*," Beal complained. He started pacing the room. "What are Bill and I supposed to do while you're running around inside Central? Assuming you survive and get in."

"The hard part," Timmorey gloated. "Sneak through the bounty-happy-bopper infested streets, to the front doors of Central and involve yourselves in diversionary actions. You can do anything you want, *except* kill Calooh."

"How long should we allow you before *we* enter?" Beal asked.

"Do you think you can make it in an hour? It might not take me that long, but it might take longer. You give me an hour," Timmorey decided, "then flood in all over the place."

The Dalph entered, carrying the equipment and some old temple clothes for Bill and Beal.

Bill wondered why Beal did whatever Timmorey said, instead of vice versa. He was becoming confused and Timmorey had already passed through the curtain with his bundle of fire gear.

Beal was slipping into a blue tunic and slacks. He

pointed to the second suit. "Put that on quickly!" he ordered.

Bill started to voice his confusion, but decided to wait. "These suits been deloused?" he demanded.

The Dalph nodded, with a reassuring smile, but he also shrugged.

Bill growled and gave the tunic and slacks a thorough inspection. When he didn't discover any wildlife, he shucked his baggy Earth togs and crawled into the Temple garb. He tweaked his ear lobe. "All set," he said, half cheerfully.

The Dalph cleared his throat. "You'll have trouble getting about," he said. "Calooh's just shut the city's power off, and the masses are all over the avenues. Some of them are getting nasty. Most are headed here because of our private generators. So, you'll have less stress, the further from the temple you progress."

"Right," Beal said. He handed Bill a heat gun. "Stuff this into your pants and be careful!"

Bill inserted the pistol in his waist band near his left hip, covering the handle with the tunic tail. He speared Beal with a poison look. "What are you afraid I'll shoot?" he said.

"Your kneecap," Beal said, "to fligg out of this mission." He bade his brother good bye with a wave and led the way into the main room.

The people pressed closer together, an almost im-

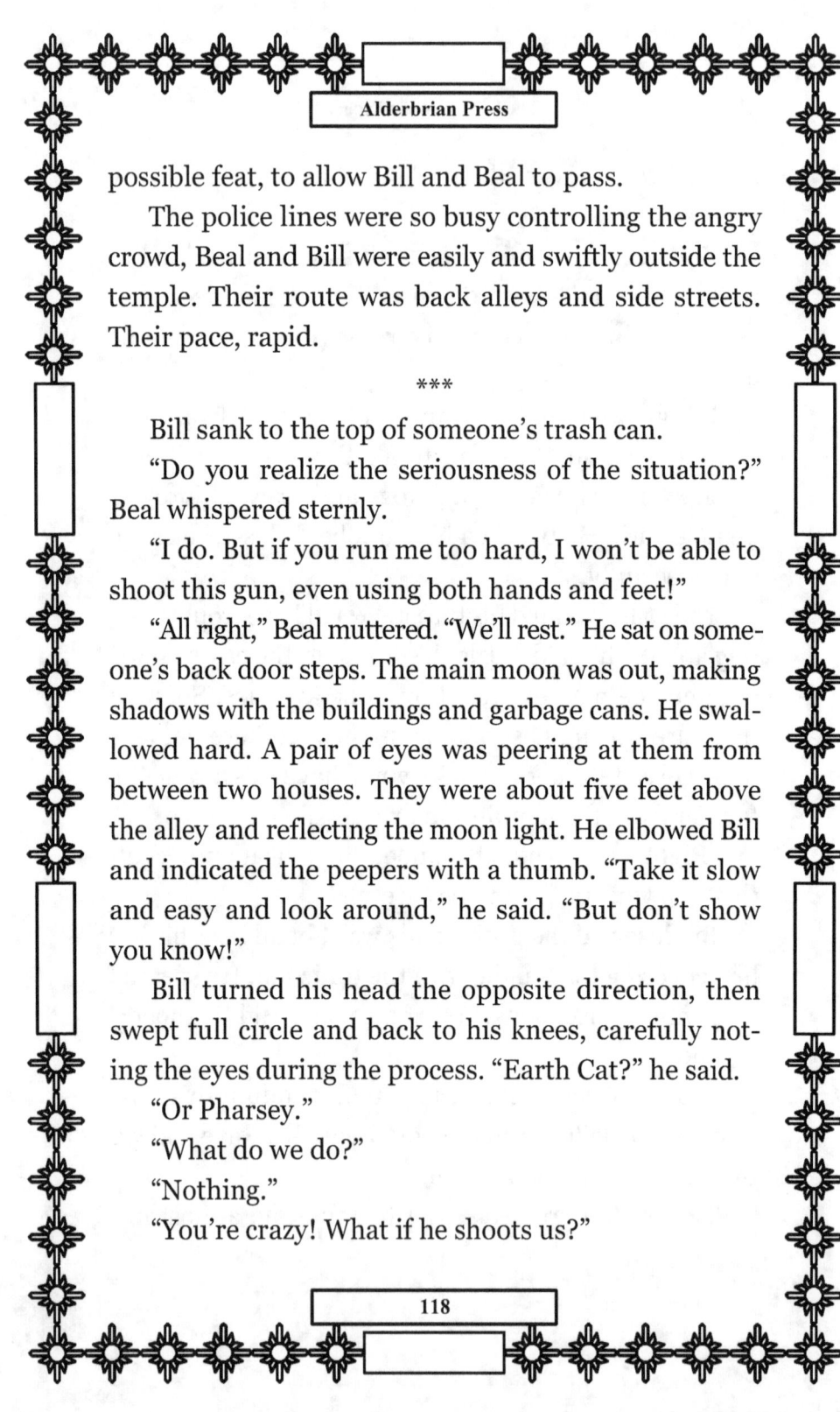

possible feat, to allow Bill and Beal to pass.

The police lines were so busy controlling the angry crowd, Beal and Bill were easily and swiftly outside the temple. Their route was back alleys and side streets. Their pace, rapid.

***

Bill sank to the top of someone's trash can.

"Do you realize the seriousness of the situation?" Beal whispered sternly.

"I do. But if you run me too hard, I won't be able to shoot this gun, even using both hands and feet!"

"All right," Beal muttered. "We'll rest." He sat on someone's back door steps. The main moon was out, making shadows with the buildings and garbage cans. He swallowed hard. A pair of eyes was peering at them from between two houses. They were about five feet above the alley and reflecting the moon light. He elbowed Bill and indicated the peepers with a thumb. "Take it slow and easy and look around," he said. "But don't show you know!"

Bill turned his head the opposite direction, then swept full circle and back to his knees, carefully noting the eyes during the process. "Earth Cat?" he said.

"Or Pharsey."

"What do we do?"

"Nothing."

"You're crazy! What if he shoots us?"

"I think he's just supposed to follow."

"So?"

Beal stood up and stretched. "We'll just have to lose him somewhere, then double back quickly," he said.

"What if he has an auto listening-tracking device homed-in on our bio-stats?"

Beal shrugged, watching the eyes carefully from the periphery of his vision. "We'll just have to char him," he said. "You move to the right. I'll fade left. When I give the word, we'll cross fire."

The peepers stood their ground without blinking.

Bill got his can off the can and took a step forward.

"Get back here!" Beal snapped. "He doesn't have one!"

Bill reached into his pants pocket as though he were searching for something. When he didn't find it, he went to Beal. "How do you know?" he said.

"If he had an ear-mounted tracker," Beal said, "he would have fled the moment I mentioned killing him. You *know* that." He slipped his hand into his slacks pocket and handed over a small, imaginary something.

Bill popped the bogus something into his big mouth. "Let's move toward him and see if he fades off," he suggested.

"Okay."

The eyes stayed where they were, without blinking.

"It must be one of the white Pharsey Officers,"

Beal said. "We could use him as a ticket to Calooh." He drew his gun surreptitiously. "Rush him!"

They ran, jumped over a row of garbage cans and rebounded off the house.

Bill lay on the cold alley cobblestones, laughing silently.

Beal snorted with disgust.

The poster showed a woman reclining on a mattress. The caption read: Sleeping on a Gertie Gretchin's Wonder Bed is just as GOOD as snoozing in PARADISE! The eyes were the os in the word, GOOD, painted so they reflected even the smallest amount of light.

"If we aren't two of the most grossly stupid—"

"Shhhhhh!" Bill said. He scrambled up and peered around the corner of the house.

Beal was beside him in a moment. "What is it?" he said.

"Police patrol coming our way," Bill said. "We'd better head the other direction!"

"Right!" Beal said. He led the way across the moonlit court yard, then between two more houses.

A can rattled down a nearby walkway, bringing the boppers shouting and running.

At a moment of rare inspiration, Bill preceded Beal down a manhole in the street they were crossing. Beal pulled the lid tight seconds before two policemen raced over it.

Chapter 17

Flowing Red Death

Timmorey turned left from the beaded curtain and made his way along that wall until he reached a round metal door. He tugged it open, shoved his fire gear through, climbed in, and hauled the portal shut.

He shined his flashlight around the huge concrete pipe to find a red arrow. The green words painted beneath it read:

MAIN TUNNEL TWO TURNS LEFT.
STRAIGHT THROUGH SECTOR ONE.

He hefted the bundle to his shoulder, clutched the boomerang and flashlight in the other hand and started sloshing through the shallow, smelly water. He came to the first branching tunnel and sent the flash beam down it.

A form, standing close to a wall, ran away from the light and dodged into a pump chamber.

Timmorey grunted. It had appeared humanoid. But he had seen some uncanny life forms while traveling with Beal. Even human-sized, half man, half rat crea-

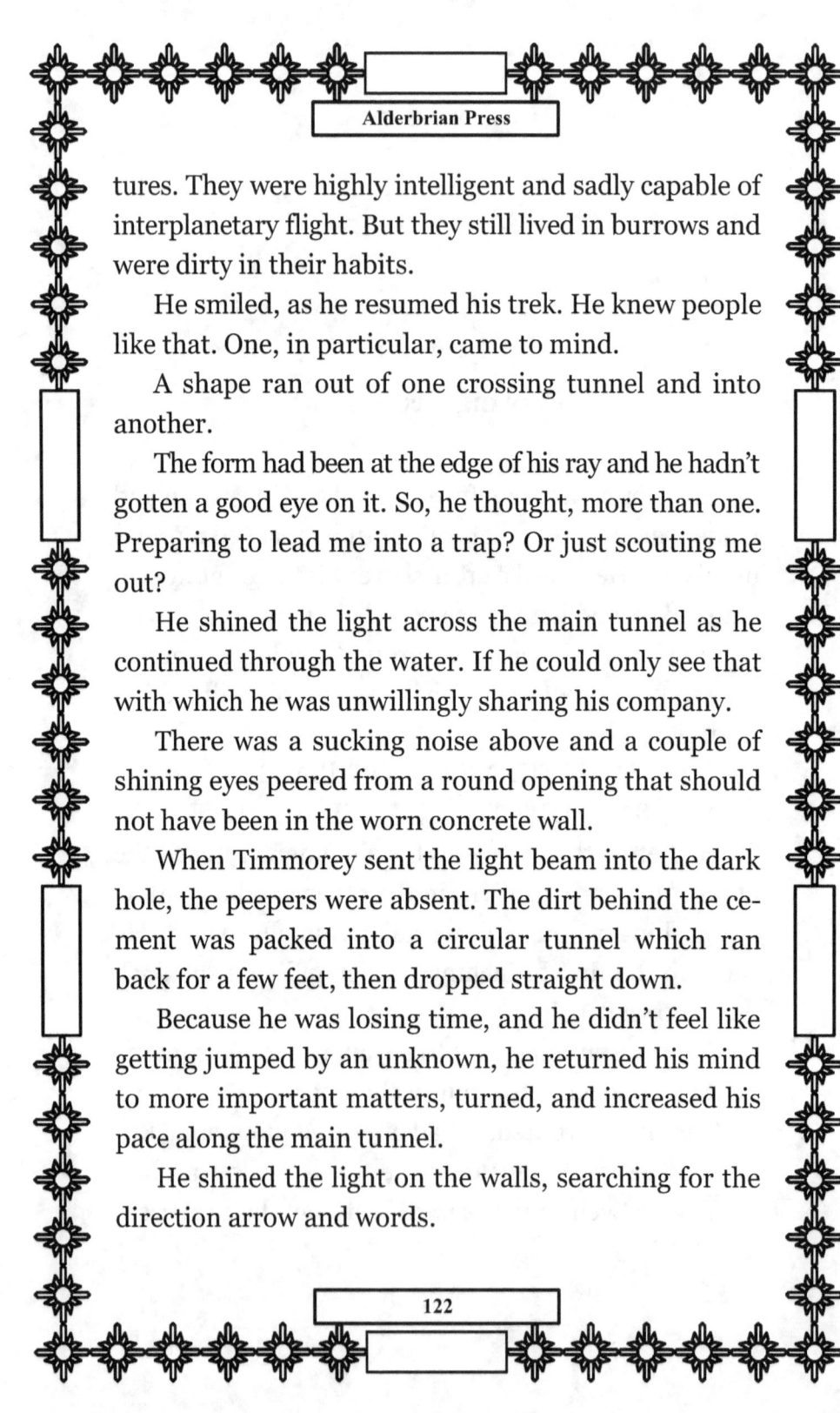

tures. They were highly intelligent and sadly capable of interplanetary flight. But they still lived in burrows and were dirty in their habits.

He smiled, as he resumed his trek. He knew people like that. One, in particular, came to mind.

A shape ran out of one crossing tunnel and into another.

The form had been at the edge of his ray and he hadn't gotten a good eye on it. So, he thought, more than one. Preparing to lead me into a trap? Or just scouting me out?

He shined the light across the main tunnel as he continued through the water. If he could only see that with which he was unwillingly sharing his company.

There was a sucking noise above and a couple of shining eyes peered from a round opening that should not have been in the worn concrete wall.

When Timmorey sent the light beam into the dark hole, the peepers were absent. The dirt behind the cement was packed into a circular tunnel which ran back for a few feet, then dropped straight down.

Because he was losing time, and he didn't feel like getting jumped by an unknown, he returned his mind to more important matters, turned, and increased his pace along the main tunnel.

He shined the light on the walls, searching for the direction arrow and words.

There was a slithering.

He whipped around with the flash to catch a dark figure landing on the sewer floor beneath the high circular opening he had inspected. It scrambled, or slid, to its—was it feet—and vanished away from him, into the irritating darkness.

"It was five feet tall!" he told himself. "Is it one of those saucer-flying, brainy rats?" He shrugged, turned around and continued trotting and listening intently.

***

Timmorey finally found the vital direction arrow he was seeking and veered left. The red legend painted on the wall read:

OPERATIONS CENTRAL REFUSE OUTLET.
DANGER!
ALL REPAIRS MUST BE PERFORMED
WHILE WEARING HEAT-RESISTANT GEAR!

He untied the awkward bundle and pulled the thick rubbery pants on. As he slipped into the coat, he glanced over his shoulder.

Twenty pairs of different colored glowing eyes stared back from the dark tunnel. An unholy stench filled the sewer. It was the unique odor of a backed up septic tank.

Timmorey slapped the oxygen recycling helmet over his head to shut out the stink and zipped up the coat. The flap for the zipper sealed itself, and the bottom of the coat sealed to the waist of the pants. He slipped his booted feet into the rubbery boots, tucking the tops inside the legs of the pants, and waited for them to seal. He set the boomerang and light on a service ledge and pulled on the self-sealing, protective gloves. He waved at the peepers, and entered the steamy refuse tunnel. His flashlight and boomerang were in his other hand.

None of the eyes followed.

The temperature began to rise quickly.

Timmorey could see a dull red glow.

The steam began to turn pink.

He could now feel the heat through the suit.

Before long, he was stepping gingerly to avoid wads of molten rubbish.

Soon it became nearly impossible to miss the growing piles of glowing glop so he just slogged through them and his feet began to know the real meaning of heat through both sets of boots.

When he was five or six yards from the pipe outlet, the goop grew much thinner from extreme temperature.

The pipe was set at the top of an inclined concrete ramp. He began climbing, fighting the downward rush of the glop.

Each time he managed to gain a few steps, he would slip, slide and find himself back at the bottom of the incline. Just his misfortune; the converters had been turned on full.

He broke the seal between the coat and the pants, stuck his light and boomerang inside his jeans at his waist, allowed the suit to reseal, and wound up crawling up the ramp as best he could. He found some gaps in the cement and held into them, pulling himself along until he could get a good hold on the edge of the huge pipe.

He groaned. The pipe also sloped up. He clung to it, fumbled for a stance, and managed to hook one boot toe into one of the gaps. He stuck his head into the mouth of the pipe.

There were hoop hand holds along the topside and the pipe was only half filled with the flowing red death. He reached in, grabbed one of the hoops, and pulled his legs after him through the mess. His suit was becoming unbearable from the heat. The goop was just below his waist.

Slowly, he hauled himself up to a joint. The second pipe was large enough to slip into, but he had no idea what was at its end. He poked his head in. There seemed to be a drop off not far away.

Well, he thought, I can go in at least to the edge of the drop off. If I don't like what I see, I can always slide back into hell and continue up the original pipe.

He pressed his hands against the sides of the second pipe. Moving them inches at a time, he managed to make his way up, grateful to be out of the flowing red death.

He reached the drop off point, found out he was at the end of the pipe, and hung out of it, looking down at a vat of water. Or *was* it water? He pried his head protector off with one hand and sniffed. As far as he could tell, it *was* water. What else could it be? He teetered on the edge of his perch, fumbled for a better hold, and lost the helmet. It bobbed around on the liquid, then capsized and sank. He watched its distorted image.

Well, he thought, it isn't acid, or the helmet would have been dissolved by now. Unless this suit is acid-proof as well.

He broke the seal between the protective jacket and pants, drew his boomerang out and dropped it into the vat. He knew, for a fact, shellacked wood was not acid proof. The boomerang resurfaced and floated about undamaged.

He pitched over and sliced into the ice cold water. He swam around, allowing the suit to cool, retrieved his helmet and boomerang, then paddled to a hoop ladder where he climbed up, then down the respective sides of the vat.

He peeled the suit off and shoved it into the space between the wall and the vat. He considered the flashlight, then discarded it, keeping only the boomerang.

The room held another equally large vat and a hulking block of blue steel. This, he guessed, was where the red hot glop was born. A door stood just beyond. He pulled it open a crack.

A muscular, hairy man stood with his back to the door. It appeared he had his arms crossed over his bare chest. He was wearing purple slacks and brown, moccasin-like shoes. He was intently watching a holo-television screen.

Timmorey felt the man was dirty *and* familiar. He jerked the door wide and walked through. "Of *all* the black holes in the *Galaxy!*" he said.

The gargantuan swung around, lifting his hands in the boxing position. His eyes actually bulged. "Oh! No!" he lamented. "How the *Clyde* did *you* get in *here*?"

"Killroy, you ugly son of a—"

"None of that, *youngster!*" Killroy said. "I suppose you've appeared to aid me with my arduous endeavors?" He turned the holo-television off, crossed his iron band arms over his burly chest, and confronted Timmorey. "Or, don't you *approve* of what I'm doing?"

"What *are* you doing?"

"I've been de-materializing these gutless birds with my porta-ray machine and re-materializing them in a sub basement where they can't do any harm. There's no way out of that trapdoor over yonder, unless you possess a Magnetic Transmit Key. *I* have the *only* one," Killroy said. "And *you* can't have it! So don't *beg!*" He laughed with delight. "Raying up his guards, one by one, is scaring the daylights outta that Calooggh. But he's got smart, he has, and yelled for his daddy quack, Faydron, to send aid. The old pluck's coming, his *damn* self. I'm saving Calooggh for last, so as you can yak at him a while."

"You're becoming intelligent," Timmorey said. Then he frowned with deep disapproval. "I haven't seen you in *two* years! You sent a bare note saying you were going away on something *big*. After that, every once in a while, a message announcing you were okay and still investigating, came in. I wasn't sure if you were *alive* for the past *year*. I guess it was too much to ask: *keep in touch!*" He sat on the television. It creaked with complaint. "You're going to have some *tall* explaining to do after we are finished here, *mister!*" He pointed an accusing digit. "You're *not* setting a shining example!"

"Yes, *mom*," Killroy said. "If you're *finished*, I'll show you the very fastest way to Calooggh."

"You'd better."

They headed through the double main doors. Twenty of Calooh's guards rounded a corner. Fire spat from their rude blasters. The men dived back into the Refuse Room.

"You must a made a lot a noise blundering in here, *junior*," Killroy accused. He fished a small electronic key from his slacks pocket and tapped the end against one of the doors to engage the lock. "How *did* you sneak in here?"

"Via the sewer."

"The what?"

"The *sewer*," Timmorey repeated, enjoying Killroy's expression of amazement. "Is there *another* way out of here?"

"The *sewer*," Killroy said. "The way *you* came in." The doors became red in the center and he retreated. "The *sewer*," he marveled. "Is that *right*?" He reached into his other pocket and pulled out a smashed pack of cigarettes. He held them up. "Smoke?"

"Don't you know, smoking causes—Iges?"

"I thought they discovered a cure for that twenty years ago," Killroy said, "before *you* were as tall as *my* knee." He tugged a silver tube from the same pocket, lit the fag, then shoved the tube and pack back into their resting place.

"Not on Mother Earth," Timmorey said, "Which, in spite of hair-brained policy, *will* be rectified." He watched the red spot on the doors increase in girth. "We're going to have to plan some kind of fight for when they burst in here. Unless those doors melting is one of *your* defense strategies."

Killroy blew smoke at him. "Don't be absurd, *boy*!" he said. "That's more *your* style."

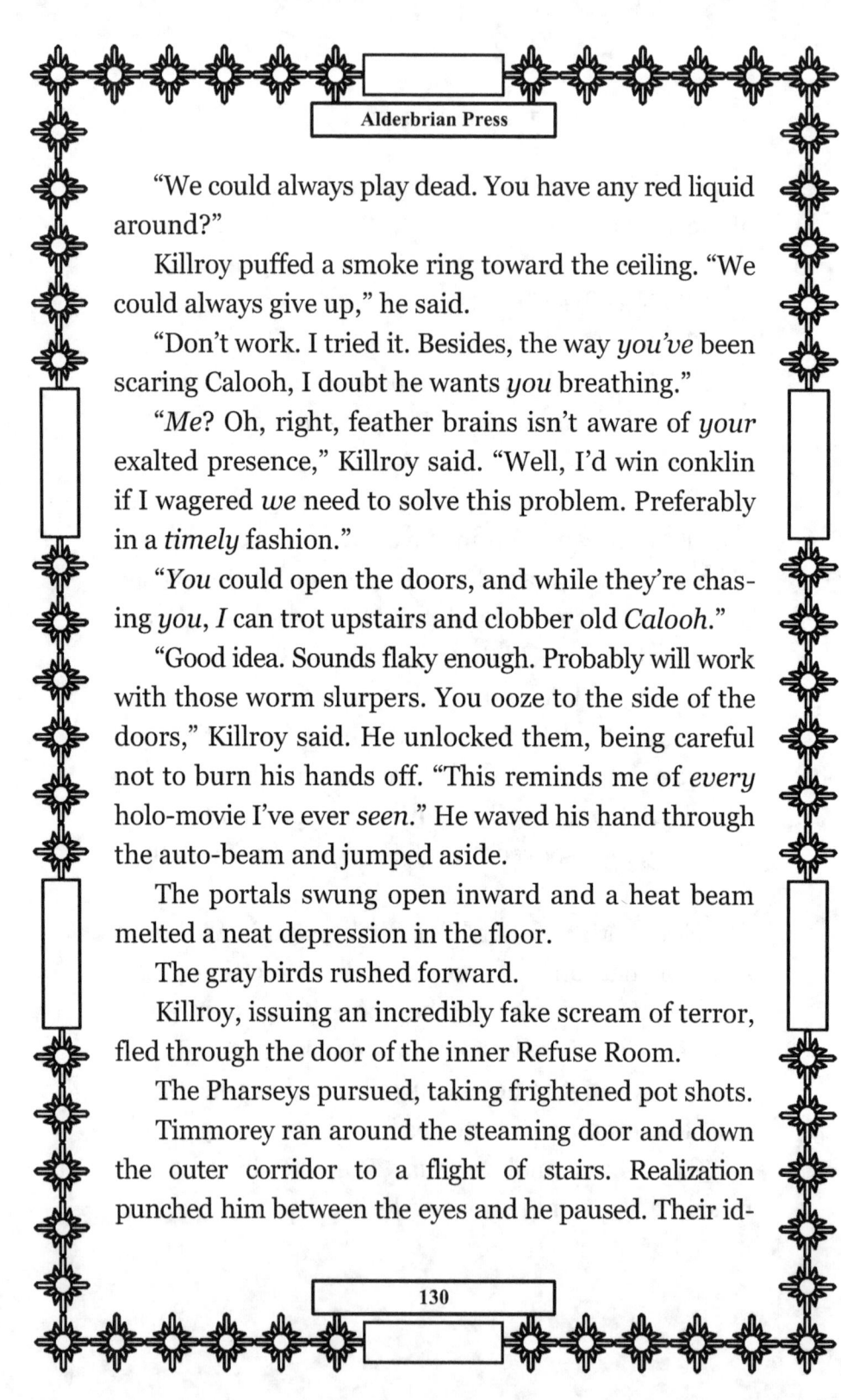

"We could always play dead. You have any red liquid around?"

Killroy puffed a smoke ring toward the ceiling. "We could always give up," he said.

"Don't work. I tried it. Besides, the way *you've* been scaring Calooh, I doubt he wants *you* breathing."

"*Me?* Oh, right, feather brains isn't aware of *your* exalted presence," Killroy said. "Well, I'd win conklin if I wagered *we* need to solve this problem. Preferably in a *timely* fashion."

"*You* could open the doors, and while they're chasing *you*, I can trot upstairs and clobber old *Calooh*."

"Good idea. Sounds flaky enough. Probably will work with those worm slurpers. You ooze to the side of the doors," Killroy said. He unlocked them, being careful not to burn his hands off. "This reminds me of *every* holo-movie I've ever *seen*." He waved his hand through the auto-beam and jumped aside.

The portals swung open inward and a heat beam melted a neat depression in the floor.

The gray birds rushed forward.

Killroy, issuing an incredibly fake scream of terror, fled through the door of the inner Refuse Room.

The Pharseys pursued, taking frightened pot shots.

Timmorey ran around the steaming door and down the outer corridor to a flight of stairs. Realization punched him between the eyes and he paused. Their idiot ploy had *worked*! "Take the elevator!" he shouted, as loud as he could, through cupped hands.

Moments later, the birds passed the stairway, toward the elevators.

Timmorey peeked through the windows of the doors which led from the stairwell to the second floor.

A Pharsey stood halfway down the hall.

Timmorey opened one door, his arm flew, and the boomerang walked the air.

Before the startled bird could ascertain the origin of the weird sound, it was knocked unconscious, and flopped to the floor, still grasping the heat gun in its small, gray hand.

The boomerang had just enough space in the ostentatious, wide hallway, to arc and return to Timmorey. He discarded it, shaking his hand in pain. "That wasn't such a notable idea," he mumbled. He crossed the corridor and pressed the UP arrow button on one of the elevator Selector panels.

They'll probably think I'm the seek and destroy team Calooh ordered into the basement, he thought. He boarded the car and tapped the appropriately numbered button.

There was a foot falling from the direction of the stairwell entrance. Killroy skidded into the elevator, just before the doors closed. "Going up?" he asked cheerfully.

"Straight down to Hell, sir," Timmorey said. "They

give green stamps."

"By all means, then," Killroy said. "Let's away!"

Clawed feet kicked the doors below. These sounds swiftly faded.

"Do you know how to impersonate a Pharsey?" Timmorey asked.

"I can eat seeds and whistle," Killroy said. "If *that's* what you mean? But that's where the similarity ends, *anyhow*!"

The elevator passed floors three and four.

"Prepare thyself, my son," Timmorey said. "Events *may* become sticky."

Killroy smiled!

Chapter 18

Sealisle

The manhole cover settled noiselessly into place. One overhead light barely illuminated the metal ladder.

Beal stepped off the last rung and bumped into Bill. "What's wrong with you?" he said, with annoyance.

"I saw a *worm*!" Bill said.

"So, what?"

"It had big, green eyes. I'd swear it went into a hole in the wall."

"How can a man get drunk without liquor?"

"I tell you, I saw a *worm*! It almost banged into me! It had four legs, kinda like tentacles, and it was running on them!"

"Have your *hallucinations* on your *own* time!" Beal said. "And don't bother *me* with them, even then. *Get going*!"

"*No*! Let's climb out of here *before* that worm comes back! No telling what it might do!"

"If it returns, step on it!"

"But, it's *five feet tall*!" Bill almost shouted. "How

you gonna squash a hundred pounds of worm with even your immense foot?" He headed up the ladder.

Beal reached out to stop Bill but caught sight of a pair of glowing green eyes. He changed the direction of his hand, intending to prove the peepers were os, like on the alley poster, remembered he was in a sewer, and felt warm, living, slimy skin. He wiped his hand on his slacks and mounted the metal ladder. As he closed the lid, the eyes were watching. "You were right, Bill!" he said. "Let's move!"

They followed the street toward another.

A manhole cover lifted and the worm stuck up out of the dark sewer. It blinked its green eyes. It had two oval nose holes and a slit like mouth. "Heeelooo," it said.

"Hi," Bill said nervously.

"Will you talk with me?"

"We're in a hurry," Beal said. "Can you wait a few hours?"

"We need to speak with you *now*," the worm said. "We *cannot* wait." It easily shoved the heavy manhole cover all the way back with the rear of its head area and climbed out of the sewer to stand on four thin tentacles.

Bill noticed a tentacle on both sides of, and halfway down, the worm's body. Each had five smaller tentacles at the end, arranged something like fingers.

"Sorry," Beal said. "But it *has* to be later."

Five worms emerged from a manhole behind.

Bill saw them. "The Universe is dying!" he shouted at the green-eyed worm. "If you keep us any longer, it might be too *late* to prevent it!"

"We understand! We can help!" the worm said. "*Please!*" It swayed back and forth with urgency. "If you want to *save* the Universe, come after me!" It leaped into the sewer.

"Let's *go!*" Beal ordered.

"I don't *like* it!" Bill protested. "Timmorey may *need* us!"

"Don't kid yourself," Beal said. "He'll do better without our aid. Besides, there's someone at Central who'll give him all the assistance he can stand." He followed after the worm.

Bill looked around. The other worms had vanished and the lid of the manhole they had used was closed. After a moment of indecision, he climbed down the ladder, drawing the cover into place.

The green-eyed guide was glowing pink, lighting the sewer enough for everyone to see to walk.

Bill's voice echoed off the cement. "Are you *sure* about this?" he said.

"The worm was sincere," Beal said. "He has something he knows will ease the situation."

Bill shrugged, reluctantly trusting Beal's hunch, instincts, or mega wild imagination.

The worm came to a hole in the sewer wall and led

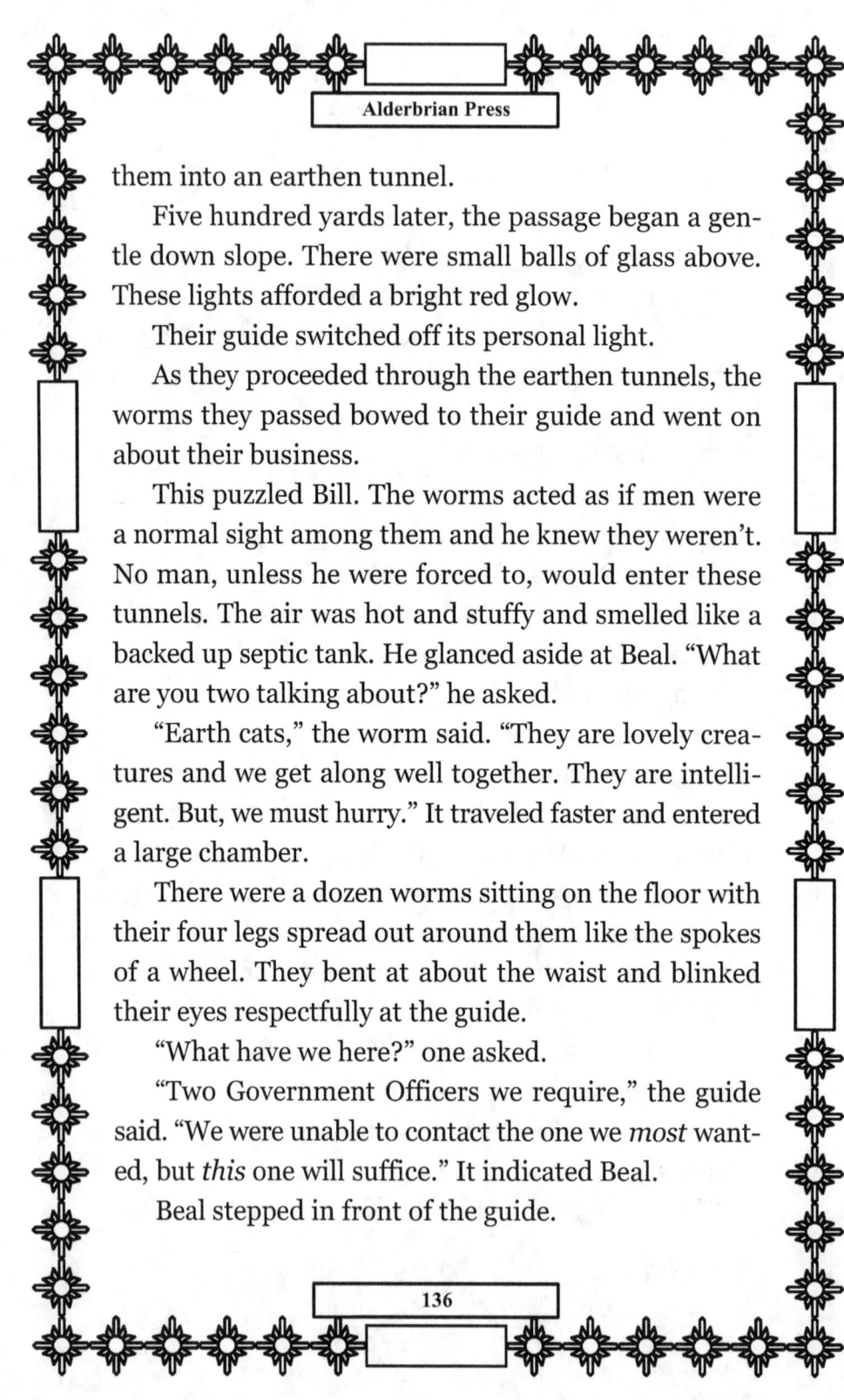

them into an earthen tunnel.

Five hundred yards later, the passage began a gentle down slope. There were small balls of glass above. These lights afforded a bright red glow.

Their guide switched off its personal light.

As they proceeded through the earthen tunnels, the worms they passed bowed to their guide and went on about their business.

This puzzled Bill. The worms acted as if men were a normal sight among them and he knew they weren't. No man, unless he were forced to, would enter these tunnels. The air was hot and stuffy and smelled like a backed up septic tank. He glanced aside at Beal. "What are you two talking about?" he asked.

"Earth cats," the worm said. "They are lovely creatures and we get along well together. They are intelligent. But, we must hurry." It traveled faster and entered a large chamber.

There were a dozen worms sitting on the floor with their four legs spread out around them like the spokes of a wheel. They bent at about the waist and blinked their eyes respectfully at the guide.

"What have we here?" one asked.

"Two Government Officers we require," the guide said. "We were unable to contact the one we *most* wanted, but *this* one will suffice." It indicated Beal.

Beal stepped in front of the guide.

The seated worms became agitated, muttering to one another in their soft, hiss-like, natural language.

"Can you come to the point quickly?" Beal said.

"*Please*, sir," the guide protested, "we do not understand *all* of your customs, and we do have *ours*!"

"One," a resting worm stated, "is *never* to walk ahead of the *King*!"

Beal moved aside. "I seek the King's *pardon*," he said. "But I still think we are wasting precious time!"

"You are correct," the King said. He waved a tentacle ended tentacle.

The seated worms sprang up to the tips of their walking tentacles and filed through one of the two tunnels facing them.

The King led Bill and Beal down the other. "My Council precedes directly beside me," he explained.

Bill peered into the red-tinted distance. "Where *are* we headed?" he said. "I don't see any way you can help."

"Be patient," the King chided, "for we are going to an object of great awe. It is something the Universe needs dearly."

"An *Item*!" Bill exclaimed. "You have an *Item*!"

The King nodded. "You call it an Item, we use another name," he said. "But, I believe it is not the type to which you are accustomed."

They traveled through a maze of tunnels.

Bill rubbed his head. "Timmorey must have gotten

into Central by now," he said. "I wonder how he's do-ing?"

"I have confidence in him," Beal said, with a secre-tive expression. "He'll get in and pump what he wants out of Calooh."

"Ahh, the Pharsey," the King said. "His father, Fay-dron, has landed with a sizable armed squadron. I'm afraid they are on their way to your Operations Cen-tral now. It will soon be hard for anyone to pass in or out. I would venture to say, impossible."

"How do you know this?" Beal said. He was begin-ning to wonder whether he had made the correct deci-sion in following the King into the heart of his people.

"I have listeners all over the Galaxy. Or, at least, in the Unified Planetary Systems," the King said. "I find out about every important event, sooner or later. More often sooner."

"But how?" Beal asked.

"Ten years ago, we sent one of our invisibility-masked saucers to establish a teleporter base, then beamed in," the King said. He chuckled in an almost Human man-ner. "We have been seen. But each time, your people thought they were very intoxicated, became even more so, and did not report us. We are not pretty to you, as you are not to us."

Bill hit himself resoundingly on his forehead. "Why didn't we just use *teleporters* to get into Central?" he said.

"The only porters are in Central, Galaxy Control and the sub-station planets. You *know* that," Beal said.

"All right," Bill said. "But *I* got splikked to Earth, *from* the Temple of Thought, *somehow*. Can you explain *that*?"

"It's just supposed to be a receiver," Beal said. "I don't know how it was crossed."

The King twisted the top half of his body around. "My best electro-tech was working with that porter just a few minutes before Bill ran into the beam and tripped the device," he said. "That porter was set to dispatch one person to earth, then to revert to a normal receiver. It was a test of some of our new technology."

"Too coincidental," Beal accused.

"All right," the King confessed, with a smile on his slit-like lips. "My electro-tech was underground and awaiting Bill. When we discovered Calooh had made his move against you, and Bill had been jailed and escaped to the Temple, we figured sending him to Earth would be an excellent way of informing Timmorey of your plight and of getting him to handle this vital situation himself. Oh," the King added. "Killroy's last message said Timmorey had arrived safely in Central."

Bill was as lost as the navel on a five thousand pound man. "What *are* you talking about?" he said. "You sound as if all this was *planned*?"

"*Foreseen*," the King said.

Both men elevated their eyebrows in surprise.

They arrived at a sizable earthen antechamber. There was a black curtain blocking the main room from sight.

The Council worms were filing into the antechamber from the second tunnel.

The King indicated the cloth with a tentacle ended tentacle. "The Item is there," he said.

Beal approached the barrier.

Bill drew his gun, making sure the worms couldn't see it.

Beal yanked the cloth aside along its rod and gasped. "My Stoth!" he said.

"Yes!" the King agreed.

Bill just stared.

The Item was twenty feet in circumference and half buried in the moist, ebony earth. It was humming softly, and glowing deep, purple-black.

Beal caressed the Item with a tender hand.

The humming became louder.

"It acknowledges your touch," the King said. "It holds fantastic might, yet it needs the aid of less powerful beings such as you and I."

"How can *we* help?" Bill asked.

"Ten years ago, in the middle of the night," the King said, "it burrowed into an empty field, next to the city, until it reached our nest. I was here when it appeared, and I at once realized what it was. I had thoughts of filling up the cavity, but, as I looked, the ceiling pulled itself together and hardened. When my people checked, the surface was as it had been before the landing, even to the smallest detail. I stayed with the Sealisle for months before I understood it was attempting to speak. When we established contact, it alerted me to the Strain, then began amassing energy. But, there is a grave problem."

"Hasn't it the power needed?"

"Yes, Mr. Beal, but *only* for the Strain repair," the King said." It says the Strain has worsened beyond its calculations. It cannot wait to gain more energy. It cannot dig itself free, because this would require too much of its might. The healing of the Strain would then be jeopardized, even if other Items were to help." He waved a tentacle tipped tentacle. "We cannot teleport it, because the porter energy would neutralize the Sealisle's power. And we have neither the tools nor the energy sources to dig it out. This is why we have contacted you."

Beal concentrated for a moment. "What buildings are over it now?" he asked.

"Only one of importance," the King said. "The Holy Temple of Thought."

Beal went into a frown. Then he nodded. "Don't

worry," he told the Item, running a hand over its dark, dimpled surface, "we'll have the way cleared soon, no matter how may birds we have to fight!"

The Item hummed louder, then fell silent.

"You must go in *haste*," the King said. "My brother will guide you to the Temple, through the sewers."

A worm, with one blue eye and one green eye, sprang to a standing position, waved a tentacled tentacle at the men, and trotted into one of the tunnels.

Beal shook the King's tentacle-hand. "We'll get word to you as soon as we've begun excavating," he pledged. Then he ran, with Bill, after their disappearing guide.

Chapter 19

The Old Noise

The elevator jolted to a stop, but the doors remained closed.

"I've trapped you now, you egg-eating, no-feathers!" Calooh gloated from the hallway. "I have a lock on the outer doors and stops to prevent you from going up or down. There is a bomb lying beside me, and it is set to explode twenty minutes after I've beamed to Earth. I would like to watch you die, but I will forgo that pleasure to procure your Item! I hope you appreciate my allowing you to expire swiftly!"

There was a sadistic cackling, then many clawed feet tapped across the tiles, fading toward their right.

"Now, what?" Killroy asked, as he checked the walls of the elevator.

"Exactly what you're doing," Timmorey said. He jumped onto Killroy's shoulders, piggyback, and grasped a metal beam just below the elevator ceiling. He felt around the large lighting squares. "No escape hatch!" he said, with disbelief. "*We* have sense enough to use

those on *Earth*."

"Tell it to blustery Beal."

Timmorey tested the cross bar by twisting it up and down. One side was loose. "When I say to, pull."

"This is not the way to get taller," Killroy observed.

"It's cheap. Pull!"

Both men strained. The left end of the beam gave out and they tumbled to the floor.

Timmorey rolled off Killroy and stood up. He yanked on the cross bar until the right end broke free. He jammed one end between the doors and heaved toward himself, using his weight in the levering action. Killroy helped by pushing against Timmorey's chest. The lock creaked, cracked and broke, and all the doors whispered open.

Timmorey dropped the beam in the elevator. He and Killroy approached the bomb in the center of the corridor. It was homemade, but powerful enough to blow the elevator, and half the hallway, into smoking ruins.

Killroy squatted and traced the wiring with his practiced eyes: from the power cell to the explosive. "This is gonna be a hard 'un," he said. "It's got back wash built in. You're gonna have to assist the Bomb Doctor, *Mr. Nurse.*"

"Do what?" Timmorey asked, as he gazed down the hall. "That's good. You take care of it." He left at a fast walk.

Killroy snorted with disgust, then ran his fingers gingerly along the double set of wires, with his hands moving away from each other.

Timmorey returned and knelt beside him. "What was it you wanted?" he said.

"What happened to *you*?" Killroy asked. He pointed to one of the sets of wires. "Take hold of those at both ends and yank when I say. We have to *go* at the same time, or we'll both *go* at the same time. Okay?"

"I was reconnoitering, *Mr. Eloquence.*"

"Pull!"

There was a dull explosion.

Timmorey nodded. "Find out what that was," he said, "then meet me at the teleporters."

Killroy charged along the hall and ran down the stairwell, four steps at a time.

Timmorey trotted along the corridor to the right of the elevator they had exited. He reached a large room which did not seem to have a door. The walls were covered with knobs, wheels and small, glowing lights.

A closed iron portal stood opposite the main entrance. He walked over and pushed it open. Ten glass booths, each four feet per side and nine feet tall, stood in the center of the bare-walled Teleporter Room.

Timmorey backed out of the Porter Room and inspected the myriad rows of lights. He found the bulb he desired: Sub-Station Earth. It changed from white to green. He approached the iron door with a fist raised.

Killroy entered from the hallway, breathing hard. He glanced at the teleporter bulbs. "Somebody beaming in, huh," he said. "The Refuse Room blew its crown. Probably because of those bird's pot shotting at *me*. It took some of the first floor and half of the street. Nobody got hurt, I don't think. You still want that bird *alive*?"

"Yes. Hold still." Timmorey swung the door open wide so it caught in that position.

The chamber on the right end of the row of porters, clouded up. Two shapes appeared and the mist evaporated.

"Alan! Laura! No!" Timmorey said, with dismay. He ran to the booth and snapped the door open.

"Timmorey!" Alan shouted, with surprise and relief.

"What *happened*?" Timmorey asked. "How did you get *sent* here?"

"I—I'm not sure," Alan said. "Laura and I were outside your cabin, with your supplies, waiting for you and your cousin. The door opened suddenly and some big, pug-ugly, white bird-thing was standing there. It screamed in rage when it saw us, and a bunch more different colored birds poured out of your—closet." He shook his head. "I don't see how they could. You can't stuff that many —people—into a closet *that* size! Anyway, we were surrounded by gray birds holding some kind of weird guns, and were forced into the cabin. We stood a spell, while that white bird ran around cursing and throwing stuff on the floor. It found your root cellar and jumped in. When it came up, it was carrying some purple rock like it was pure gold. It set the rock on the cot and swore. Something about having to risk going outside to wait for its father's saucer, otherwise the old simpleton would be insulted. Then it gave orders we couldn't understand to our guards. They shoved us into your closet. Next thing we knew, we were here!"

"Where *are* we, Timmorey?" Laura whispered. "How did *you* get here?"

"I can't explain *now*," Timmorey said. He laid a reassuring hand on her shoulder. "You two go into the other room, with Killroy, and wait. I have to go to Earth, *quickly*!"

Alan grew pale. "What do you mean, *go* to Earth?" he said. "Are we *on* some *other* planet?"

"Yes," Timmorey said. "Check the lights, Killroy!" he shouted.

"How did *you* get involved in whatever *this* is?" Alan asked.

"Tell you later," Timmorey said. "Killroy?" He opened the door to the chamber in which Alan and Laura had arrived.

"It's all clear!" Killroy shouted. "You'll *need* a blaster!"

Bill skidded into the Teleporter Control Room. He shot Killroy an odd look, then ran into the Porter Room.

"Wait," he said. "I know where some beamers are!"

"Get 'em!" Timmorey ordered.

Bill raced into the hallway, turned left, went to the end, and entered a storage room. He shoved some wooden crates aside and fumbled with the thumb print latch of a small, round metal door in the wall. Catching up the two emergency blasters there, he made sure they were fully charged, then returned to the group. He laid the beamers on the floor by the Porter Room door.

Timmorey had gently ushered Alan and Laura into the Teleporter Control Room. He was examining the winking lights on the walls. "Stay quiet," he told everyone, "somebody's arriving."

Alan stepped forward. "I can help," he said.

"Stick close to Laura," Timmorey ordered. "And just get her the hell out of here, the best way you can, *if* anything happens."

"But—"

Timmorey walked to the Porter Room doorway and stared at the chambers.

Alan joined Laura near one of the bulb covered walls.

"Jamming," Timmorey finally muttered. He studied the lights on the wall to the left of the Porter Room doorway, then he motioned to Killroy. "He must not have found my main controls, or he would have blown these chambers. We still have a chance."

Bill nosed in. "What now?" he said.

"We wait," Timmorey said. He frowned. "Did you see any police, close by, when you entered?"

"No," Bill said. "But, they should be flooding in here, pretty soon, to see why the Refuse Room exploded. And, there's going to be a major riot, and looting, unless the power comes back on in Sector One."

Timmorey stepped to the bulbs near the Earth indicator. He followed a row to the corner on his left. He waved a hand down three feet from the top of this row, to two feet from the floor. A huge panel dropped into the doorway of the Teleporter Control Room, sealing them from all outside interference. He puzzled over the lights again. "I'm not familiar with the pattern, but I might be able to—" He waved his hands above the bulbs, in obscure angles. The ceiling panel lights changed from dim to bright. He made a few more passes. "That should do it," he said, with a chuckle. "I even turned on the Emergency Flood Lights for all Sectors."

They were startled by the sounds of many running feet outside the great door. They receded. Down the hall, both ways, sounds of doors being slammed open and furniture being knocked about, could be heard.

"The beauty of that is," Killroy purred, pointing at the gray slab, "it blends in with the wall and is nearly impossible to detect."

"Mister," Bill said to Killroy, "just who, in hell, *are*

you? I mean, you *aren't* a Janitor, like I thought, and you *know* Timmorey. *Everybody* knows Timmorey. Why didn't *I* know Timmorey? I'm not sure if the people *I* know who know Timmorey are really the people *I* know." He worked his jaws for a moment, then he shrugged. "Mega confused!" he acknowledged.

"It would help if you explained some things, Tim," Alan said. "Laura and I might not be so frightened, if we knew what we're up against."

Timmorey continued studying the lighted wall. "That gorilla squatting so smugly, there, is the head of the Galactic Security Forces. They have a hand in everything of importance going on in the Galactic Systems. Killroy usually takes on what he deems are the most urgent problems. He has a nasty habit, that *will* change, of disappearing for long periods and carrying on operations that are secret, even to the Presider of the Galactic Gathering. Or so he imagines."

Killroy was surprised and dismayed.

"Galactic Gathering," Alan marveled. "How many planets are in it?"

"So many, we have a New-York-City-sized computer to keep track of the alliances struck," Timmorey said.

"I take it," Laura ventured, "Earth hasn't been contacted by the—Gathering—of Planets because it's too far behind in everything?"

"No," Timmorey said. "Each world must have sustained one successful civilization for a regulation number of years and to have attained a certain type of political philosophy to be contacted. There are other specifications of course. Too many to mention now." He was still scrutinizing the bulbs.

"Are you *really* from Earth?"

"Yes, Bill," Timmorey said. "You can ask Alan and Laura about that. They knew my father and my mother. And their father and mother knew my parent's parents and so on, pretty far back." He raised a hand across a short row of the lights.

"About your *closet*," Laura said.

Timmorey laughed. "It's a way station for keeping order throughout the Planetary Systems. There are *millions* more like it. I had a talk with one of the Galaxy Control agents who landed outside my cabin in a saucer. He decided me to keep a porter. Of course, I did a little Interstellar traveling and learning before taking it on."

"Then, you're just one of their outpost keepers?" Laura said.

"*No,*" Bill insisted. "He's something more. *What,* I haven't figured out, *yet.* But I *intend* to. Every order he barks is executed by everyone who knows him, including Killroy. He has to be high up in the officer lists of Galaxy Control, for that. Maybe he's—"

"That's enough *wild* guessing, Bill," Timmorey ordered, in that voice Bill dearly hadn't wanted to hear again. "I'm what I seem to be, a man trying to avert a disaster." He waved a hand over another section of lights. The winking ones were extinguished, except for the small bulb designating Earth.

Killroy was appalled. "You didn't *shut* the other porters *down*?" he said.

"Just their indicator lights," Timmorey said. He gestured and half the wall to his right regained its glows. The wall to his left showed only the Earth bulb, with its steady green shine. He made a hand pass along the dark lights and the Earth bulb turned pink. "Now Calooh can't blow these chambers, unless he can jury rig my main controls."

"Timmorey, I—"

"Good," Timmorey told Bill. "You have to get back to Beal and help him out with whatever he's doing. By the way, what is, *Mr. Temper*, doing?"

Bill forgot the puzzle of Timmorey's identity as he saw a picture of the gigantic Item in his mind. He smiled. "We were trying to reach Central, like you ordered, when we ran into a group of worm-like people," he said.

"The *Sarem*!" Timmorey said. "I should have *guessed* it was the King and his people peering at me. Did he offer help?"

"You bet! And, I wish you wouldn't rudely interrupt me, whoever the hell you are," Bill said.

Killroy sniggered.

Timmorey stared at them.

Bill turned red.

Killroy winced.

"Sorry," Bill said, "sir," he added, for insurance. "But, they have the biggest, fuzzo, Item you've ever *seen*, just *itching* to tear into that Strain. The Temple of Thought is over it and it can't dig itself out of the ground without using too much of its power, and they can't teleport it, because that would negate its energy. We gotta dig it loose, some way, quickly." He took a breath. "That's not too clear, but you can catch the picture."

"How large is it?" Timmorey asked.

"Is what?" Bill said.

"The Item," Timmorey said, with a laugh. "How large was it, and did they make speech contact?"

"It was, maybe, twenty feet in circumference," Bill bubbled. "They spoke to it, but it blinked back in code. I couldn't understand it. It seemed to like Beal, though."

"What *is* Beal doing?" Timmorey said.

"He's helping his brother clear the people out of the Temple of Thought so we can rip it down," Bill said. "The boppers are getting in the way, though, still following Calooh's orders."

"You go tell Beal to forget that," Timmorey said. "It's unnecessary."

"But," Bill protested, "the Item said the other Items couldn't hold the Strain and the Strain is going to bust any time now, if it doesn't get at it, slick-fast!"

Timmorey continued watching the wall lights. "Don't argue," he warned, in that tone Bill didn't like.

Alan and Laura looked at each other for reassurance and shrugged at the incomprehensible conversation.

"It's hard to *believe* we're *on* another planet," Laura said. "But if Tim says *so*, I guess we *are*."

"Don't worry," Alan said. "I'm not sure how important Tim is, but I know he'll take care of us."

"Do you think we can look around this world some?" Laura whispered.

"Guess we'll have to ask Tim."

Timmorey escorted Bill to the open Porter Room door and said: "The fourth chamber. I'll be able to send you there, but you and Beal will have to find your own way back. Tell him I said, *no! I'll* think of something else."

There was a clamor in the hallway. The steady buzzing of heat pistols followed and the center of the great door began to glow red.

Timmorey touched some bulbs and a holo-television set popped out of the the middle of the floor. It showed Territorial Policemen doing the beaming. He stormed over to the dark wall and pressed a palm over six blue-colored, unlit bulbs. A panel slid open by the Earth Designator light and revealed a radio microphone on a shelf. He lifted it and depressed the transmit button on its stem with the same motion. "Galaxy Control," he said icily, "this is Alderbrian speaking!"

"Galaxy Control here, your identity is verified via your Vital Signs Telemetry Unit. Proceed with message." The man's voice came from a speaker inside the microphone niche.

"I am in Operations Central Teleportation Control Center," Timmorey said. "Get these local police *off* my neck! Clear this building of them *immediately*! *Imperative*! *Acknowledge*! *Out*!"

"Galaxy Control acknowledges. Out."

Bill's chin felt like it dropped to his knees.

Killroy grinned like an Earth Cheshire Cat. "That's *keeerect*!" he drawled. "He's the Old Noise! He runs the whole big, durned, misty Galaxy!"

Timmorey shot his Security Chief a murderous look and shoved the mike into its niche.

Alan and Laura were portraits of disbelief.

The buzzing of the blasters ceased. The holo-television displayed the boppers retreating at a flat out, terrified run.

Bill was working his mouth but issuing no sounds.

"Well," Killroy smirked, "you *had* to use it. Might as well *mop up* with the microphone. It's not as much *fun*, but as you know, we aren't *dripping* in excess time."

Timmorey sighed, mouthed the word, "*Nordhonger*," at Killroy, and took up the mike. "Galaxy Control," he said, "Alderbrian speaking."

"Galaxy Control here. Identity confirmed. Proceed with message."

"Directive One: Pharsey Calooh is hereby *relieved* of his position as Administrator of Operations Central. *Revoke* his *clearances* and *privileges* and *cancel* his *directives*.

"Directive Two: *Administrator Beal* is in the Temple of Thought. Inform him he is to empty and demolish the government storage buildings to the *west* of the Temple and excavate to the sewers to retrieve the Item in question. The Territorial Police and the Public Engineering Unit in Sector One, will *assist*. The Police will then escort *Administrator Beal* and new *Deputy Administrator Bill Wayden*, to their positions as legal heads of Operations Central.

"Acknowledge these directives. Out."

"Galaxy Control acknowledges. Out."

Timmorey placed the microphone in its niche, glared at Killroy, and said, "Grab one of those blasters, we're crackling to Earth to *mop* my floor with Calooh." He wrestled with Bill and shoved him into the fourth porter, which automatically beamed him to the Temple. He returned to Alan and Laura. "You wait here for Bill and Beal," he said. "They'll be back in half an hour, or so. Tell them *I* said to remain put, until we return." He reconsidered. "Until *I* return."

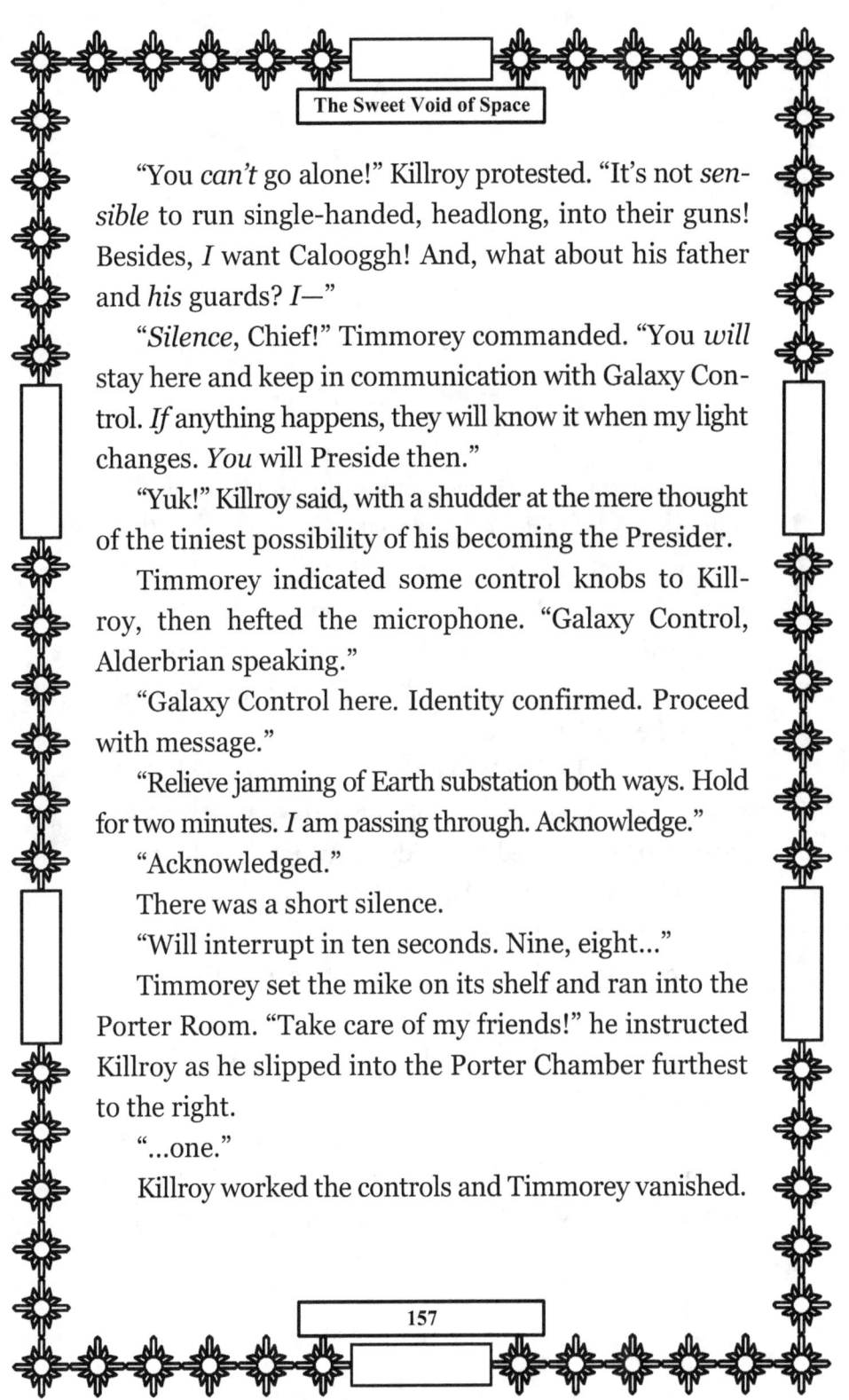

"You *can't* go alone!" Killroy protested. "It's not *sensible* to run single-handed, headlong, into their guns! Besides, *I* want Calooggh! And, what about his father and *his* guards? *I—*"

"*Silence*, Chief!" Timmorey commanded. "You *will* stay here and keep in communication with Galaxy Control. *If* anything happens, they will know it when my light changes. *You* will Preside then."

"Yuk!" Killroy said, with a shudder at the mere thought of the tiniest possibility of his becoming the Presider.

Timmorey indicated some control knobs to Killroy, then hefted the microphone. "Galaxy Control, Alderbrian speaking."

"Galaxy Control here. Identity confirmed. Proceed with message."

"Relieve jamming of Earth substation both ways. Hold for two minutes. *I* am passing through. Acknowledge."

"Acknowledged."

There was a short silence.

"Will interrupt in ten seconds. Nine, eight..."

Timmorey set the mike on its shelf and ran into the Porter Room. "Take care of my friends!" he instructed Killroy as he slipped into the Porter Chamber furthest to the right.

"...one."

Killroy worked the controls and Timmorey vanished.

Chapter 20

Calooh's Crash

Timmorey materialized in his closet. He shoved the half open door wide. A black metal box sat on the floor. This was Calooh's cheap, jamming device. Timmorey picked it up, toggled its switch off, and set it on the cot.

He felt anger at the vandalism Calooh and his guards had wreaked, but brushed it aside, keeping his mind free to better handle his duties.

Realizing he'd left the heat pistol at Central, he scooped his shotgun up from near the cot. It was still loaded. He retrieved his wide cartridge belt from the root cellar, and left the cabin, closing the door.

It was easy to sight the scratchy prints of the Pharseys. He ran into the woods, noting a broken branch here and trampled grass there. He ducked around a Maple and froze. Something ahead was breaking through brush and old tree limbs.

He ran between two Elms and into the clearing where he and Bill had visited with the rabbit. He jumped a gully and saw some white Pharseys through a gap in the trees.

Calooh was carrying the Item cradled in his wings. Three birds were with him. One was his father, Faydron. The other two were gray soldiers.

Timmorey thought: Was Faydron in on this all along? The acorn and the tree? And where are *all* those guards and slaves Alan mentioned?

"Behind us!" one of the gray Pharseys warned.

Calooh dropped the Item to the moss, grasped it in his foot claws and soared into the thick limbs of an Elm. He was joined by the other birds.

Timmorey skidded to a stop, dropped to his knee, and took aim at the group. He hesitated. They're not armed, he thought, the two grays don't have collars, and there is no smell, sight or sound of ambushers.

Calooh and Faydron exchanged irate words. There was a brief tussle between them with their foot claws.

Faydron soared toward Timmorey. "Here, Watcher!" he ordered. "Catch!"

Timmorey let the gun fall to the moss and caught the Item. He cradled it in one elbow and snatched up the shotgun.

Calooh furiously launched himself at his father. The gray guards remained in the Elm. They were too terrified by the shotgun and what they were witnessing, to even think of moving.

Timmorey realized Calooh was trying to *kill* his father. But the old bird was too crafty. He circled Calooh twice, with dizzying swiftness, hissed, dived and delivered a sharp, loud blow, with his powerful leg claws, to Calooh's back.

Calooh tumbled, stunned, to the moss.

Faydron landed by his son, grabbed him around the neck with his wing hands and jerked him to his feet.

"Please show us to your nest," the distraught father said. "When I realized his deceit, I dispatched my officers, and *this* one's group, to my saucer, with secret orders to travel to our home planet, Ziscalon. I was playing *this* one along until he divulged the whereabouts of the other Items. I trust you will retrieve my guards, when they have recovered from their shock at my son's traitorous behavior. I *will* apprise Galaxy Control of the locations of the stolen Items."

Timmorey nodded and led the way.

Calooh followed, under the vicious pecks of his father's accurate and unforgiving beak.

***

Timmorey entered his Cabin and set the Item on the stool. He looked unemotionally at the Pharseys. "Why did you assist *me*, instead of your *son*?" he asked. "Do you fully comprehend the *power* you can obtain through the Items?"

"Yes," Faydron said. "But I also comprehend the *Strain*."

"It will be taken care of by the Legend Item," Timmorey said.

"This is *excellent*!" the father said. "Had I known of this *before*, I would have acted no *differently*. I did not realize what he was doing. He told me the lies he spread on Central Control. He said he gathered the Items to personally convey them to the Strain, as a work of faith, to convince the Gathering we richly deserved full entry into the Systems. He *lied* to me in *everything*! An *unforgivable* sin for a son!" He pecked Calooh on the head. "It is *ironic*. We elders shove aside generations of ingrained traditions to become part of the Unity of the Galactic Gathering. But our mindless, upstart, fledglings rebel and accept those old ways of crime. We become *wise* and they *fall*. We are so busy prosecuting the other illegal slavers, we cannot keep watch over our *own* kin. I did not know, until today, he was using the outlawed collars on what I thought were *hired* guards and domestics! This one is ill. We think they *all* are. A son who sins against a father, and his *entire race*, is not sane! I trust he will receive treatment, medically, by judgment of the Galaxy Central Courts. *I* shall do *my* utmost to bring it about." He indicated the teleporter with one of his great wings. "We go now. Send us to Galaxy Control. I hope this incident will not cancel our Planetary Probation." He nipped and kicked Calooh into the chamber.

"You may take my word, the status of your world

shall, instead, be upgraded," Timmorey said. "The third button."

"Why do I believe you?" Faydron said, as he pecked the button.

"Because *I* am Alderbrian, and it *shall be so*," Timmorey said, with the voice which sent shivers down even Killroy's spine.

Faydron's beak fell open in astonishment.

Calooh honked hoarsely and fainted, leaning limply against his father.

The Pharseys winked out of sight.

Timmorey took the Item outside and held it out on his palms. "You are sorely needed, my friend," he whispered.

The Item hummed softly, levitated with incredible speed, and vanished into outer space.

Timmorey entered the cabin and secured the door with its wooden beam. He'd have to see about Alan and Laura, and check on the Strain. But what was he going to do about Bill? Oh, well, he thought, I'll squirm out of this some way.

***

Timmorey walked into the light bulb studded room.

Killroy stopped annoying Alan and Laura with exaggerated tales of his heroic adventures.

Timmorey gestured quickly over the correct row of bulbs and the wall door raised. He looked hopefully at

Killroy. "Is Bill around, close?" he asked.

"Naw. He ain't come back from the excavation. Where's Calooggh?"

"Galaxy Control," Timmorey gloated.

"*What*?" Killroy fumed. "You sent him there without letting me *twist* his neck even one hundred times! What kinda friend *are* you?"

"He had enough woes," Timmorey said. "His father's all but disowned him and he's in for psychiatric treatment, along with his white officers, whenever you release them from that sub-basement."

"Oh," Killroy said. He fell silent in thought.

"Well, Alan, Laura are you ready to return home?"

Alan scratched his head. "We were, err—what should we call you?" he asked.

Timmorey scowled. "Same as you've been calling me since we were born," he said.

Alan was relieved. "Okay," he said. "We were wondering if we could look around first. Would it be all right?"

"No reason why not," Timmorey said. "There isn't much to see on this planet. There are always ships bound out, however. If you want a sure eyeful, we'll get you a Grand Tour, round-trip ticket on one of those. But, *after* you're married on Earth. The tour will be a wedding gift from me, and we'll be better able to explain your absence to your folks."

Alan and Laura looked at each other and nodded eagerly.

Timmorey went to the niche and took up the mike. "Earth reminds me," he said to Alan and Laura, "I left two birds perched in an Elm tree near my cabin. You're temporary Galactic Police Officers until you help me beam them here." He thumbed the transmit button on the mike. "Alderbrian speaking," he said.

"Galaxy Control here. Your identity is confirmed. Proceed with your message."

"Any word on the grounded Item?" Timmorey asked.

"It took off twenty minutes ago, sir."

"Any problems around the Strain?"

"Two stars blew, but it was nothing serious. There were no planets in either system."

"Okay. Alderbrian, out. "Good night, there, Humphrey."

"Gee," the operator said. The boss actually knew his name. "Galaxy Control out, sir."

Beal sidled in, wearing his work clothes and cradling Fido on one arm. He shook Timmorey's hand. "Item's off fine," he said, "and the Sarem King reports everything is proceeding well. Estimates are, the Items will take two years to repair the Strain. But that's better than universal extinction."

"Where's Bill?" Timmorey asked, painfully ignoring

Beal's outrageous understatement.

"I ordered him to fill in the hole we made," Beal said, with a laugh. "I'm not sure if he took me seriously. He might be back, any moment. Hey! Why do the *Sarem* have observers by that Strain in the Fabric? And why haven't *I* ever run into a Sarem before?"

"Some of my best workers," Killroy bragged. "One thing bothers me, though. I never know where they'll show up next, just where their Command Post is. They never *tell* me anything."

"Now you know how *I* feel!" Timmorey scolded.

Killroy snorted with frustration. "All right!" he said. "You don't have to hit me over the head with a *rabid* Hounda!"

"I'll have a couple of birds for you in a few minutes," Timmorey said. "They're Calooh's father's guards and guiltless. See where he wants them sent, to him or their home planet. And *don't* forget those fowl in the subbasement."

"Handled," Killroy said. "I aim to please."

"I *won't* be back for a while," Timmorey said. "Unless you *really* need me. And don't bother to follow. I have an automatic return on my porter. I don't intend to be pulled away from my vacation again, except by radio and *real* emergencies!"

"You can't go!" Beal protested. "I haven't had any *fun* in the past week. The least you can do is eat a *Cal-burger* with me!" He glanced around for support.

Killroy shrugged. "He goes," he said. "I'll be glad to get shed of him. He's the only man I take orders from. If he barks too many at me at once, I'm liable to go plocko and pound on his head. Nice trip, boss man!"

Timmorey led Laura and Alan into the right end chamber.

Killroy sent them to Earth, then explained to Beal who Alan and Laura were.

***

Bill ran into the light bulb studded room just as the Pharseys beamed in from Earth.

"This note is for Administrator Beal," one of the birds said.

Beal smiled, handed the paper to Killroy, hooked an arm around Bill's shoulders, and led him from the room.

Killroy laughed and followed with the Pharseys.

The message read:

To: Beal

To: Killroy

Take Bill out and get him drunk.

From: A. Timmorey

***

On a primitive green planet called Earth, one of the natives sat on the shore of a lake. He had a ball of twine and an old hook. According to official Operations reports, he was fishing with no knowledge of what was really occurring in the rest of the inhabited Galaxy.

Timmorey smiled and settled into a more restful position against the trunk of a Maple tree.

www.ingramcontent.com/pod-product-compliance
Lightning Source LLC
Chambersburg PA
CBHW071214260626
47162CB00004B/1292